UNRESOLVED ISSUES

THE CHRONCLES OF CHAPTERS

PATRICK L. BROOKS

Unresolved Issues: The Chronicles of Chapters

ISBN-13: 978-1-947288-58-4

Printed in the United States of America

10 9 8 7 6 5 4 3 2 1

Cover and interior design by: Legacy Designs, Inc.
Legacydesigninc@gmail.com

Published by:
Life To Legacy, LLC
P.O. Box 1239
Matteson, IL 60443
877-267-7477
www.Life2Legacy.com

Presented to:

The Unresolved Issues Series
by
Patrick L. Brooks

Available at: UnresolvedIssues.org Amazon.com, Barnes and Noble.com, Google Books and ITunes

TABLE OF CONTENTS

Chapters

ACKNOWLEDGMENTS

I would like to give humble acknowledgements to the individuals who greatly assisted me in my physical health after enduring a traumatic injury in 2019. It was a daily grind and a slow process but the following people gave me encouragement and much support, which I greatly needed throughout the rehabbing and healing process. Dr. Michael Hejna, and Dr. Jennifer Kang, my Surgeons at Orthopedic Associates of Riverside, LLC. Thank you for your tremendous work. Thank you Donna at OAR Physical Therapy. Working with you every day gave me the strength to continue to push. You have the awesome ability to push when I needed it, and you showed great compassion when I needed that as well. I greatly Appreciate you Donna. I also want to acknowledge Maria the Administrative assistant for always providing the medical documentation needed in a timely manner, I thank you. Thank you Leslie, and Victor at MacNeal Hospital Rehab Center for going over and beyond my first day in rehab. I was distraught and uncomfortable that first day, your professionalism and willingness to go over and beyond the call of duty settled me. As a result, I completed the initial rehab that taught me how to maneuver safely up stairs. Nurse Jennifer, and Nurse's Assistant Samantha. You were great to me, I was totally dependent on you guys and my day was always better when you were present. I humbly thank you and the entire rehabilitation staff at MacNeal Hospital. God Bless you all.

SPECIAL THANKS

I give special thanks to Charlene Brooks, Patrick Jamonnie Brooks, Warren Cook, Darion Hills, Raymond Wilks Jr. and Sheena Hutchins. For being there, in my most Vulnerable moment to date. You provided me with an outpouring amount of Love and Support.

I thank My dear mother Louise Brooks-Betts for everything you put in me, that has helped manifest me into the man I am today.

Special Thanks: To My Pastors Mike and Lexa Ennis, and Broadview Wesleyan Church. Your obedience to the Word of God and your Passion for Ministry is Impressive. Apostle Paul would be Proud. Thank you for being a Blessing to our Community, and excepting me into the Wesleyan Church Family, which is what I needed at such a vulnerable period in my Life.

I give special acknowledgement to my Nephew Donte Brooks who was a major investor in the publication of this book.

I thank Dr. Dennis Woods for the special one on one attention I've received that helped to bring this book to fruition. Your efforts have not gone unnoticed and neither has your integrity.

I give exceptional acknowledgments to Monica Hayes, Kimberly McGary and Paulette McGahee. You've shown great support, by purchasing, reading and giving relevant feedback to each one of my books. Your inquiry about when the next book is being released has been fuel to the lit flame of my writing. You have truly been elite fans of the Unresolved Issues Series. Thank you.

I Love you all, along with many other Family Members, Church Members and Friends.

Throughout my physical Challenges in 2019, I was able to complete this book, and this has been some of my best writing. While enduring pain and a host of challenges, I was able to hold on to the Gift of writing. I was able to mentally escape from my current situation. In the mist of Trials I created something Special, and I give God all the Glory for the Gift he's Blessed me with, and the anointed vessels he's placed in my Life.

Lastly, but Most Importantly I want to thank Yahweh for Teaching, Providing, Healing and Loving me. I would be lost without you, but through you I can do all things!

INTRODUCTION

UNRESOLVED ISSUES; THE CHRONICLES OF CHAPTERS delves into the lives of Americans with issues of untold stories many live with. This Novel sheds light on how some have learned to embrace these issues to a place of normality in their lives. Henceforth there should be absolutely no shame in the issues of our lives that are often shaped by learned behavior and environmental adaptations. Each one of these chapters mirror a select journey through life, unaware of the culmination of what is truly reality and/or what is truly our own perception of it. The issues we possess doesn't have to be catalyst to our lives. If we take a closer look, many of us live with these issues and still manage to do well in life. Nevertheless, it is a simple matter of the way we primarily deal with the very issues we're faced with. Are we meeting them head on? Do we have the ability to identify them? Or, are we masking and ignoring the issues, which presents itself unto us.

In current news of today we've been shocked to learn role models, famous people or people we've just held in high regard, too often come to be reduced to scandals and allegations. Whether just or unjustified, it still doesn't take away from the art, the gifts or the talents that individual possesses, which may have led to the unveiling of the hidden portions of that individual's personal life altogether.

Moreover, I believe it is completely safe to assume a person can function and excel even when there is a dysfunctional part that dwells within them. The Chronicles of each Chapter of the latest collection of Unresolved Issues, illuminates and enlightens the root of both what is seen, and also what is unseen. In my professional career where I've worked with thousands of patients as a Mental Health Counselor. I've seen many clients and professionals alike faced with a host of similar issues. One person would persevere in spite of the issues, and another individual would succumb to the challenges. Perception, Perseverance and Participation were successful components I saw in those clients that didn't allow unexpected life events to stop them from having the life they had or once searched for. I've told a story hundreds of times regarding the lives of two men that were both legally blind, and how one of the men regrouped and pressed on by relying on other senses like hearing, touching and the sense of smell to be the guide of what the eyes could no longer provide. This individual overtime learned to read utilizing embroidered reading material, he learned to travel without the assistance of another human being and he maintained a social life that led to attain a romantic relationship he didn't have when he did possess sight. Unfortunately, the other man became totally dependent on others. He wouldn't take a step or maneuver even without holding on to someone to guide and direct his destination. He became bitter, angry, and very much entitled, which led him to treat others in a rude manner. This parable is really a factual observation and it coincides with how the issues that come upon us can manifest as unresolved or can be the stepping stone to a place of life fulfillment.

THE ISSUE OF *parti/ality*

CHAPTER 1

ISABELLA WAS FRUSTRATED WITH her husband Alfredo this warm spring evening, after discovering he'd left his beard trimmings in the bathroom sink this morning from his shave. Part of her frustration was also due to Alfredo waking her up when he entered their bedroom last night after working a double shift.

Alfredo was currently working as a security guard for Ignacio Security Firm. He had been assigned to a contractual construction site for the past year while a mini-mall was being built in the Humboldt Park community of Chicago. Alfredo was very good with his hands, and he could fix almost anything, especially cars. However, he was not currently working in the automotive field, because of his lack of education. Alfredo had dropped out of high school while yet a teenager himself to help his mother take care of his younger brothers and sisters. It was then that Alfredo learned many trades such as landscaping, painting, and housekeeping, and he eventually found work at an auto repair shop, cleaning the garage and the lobby area of the business. Alfredo assisted the mechanics when he wasn't consumed with his own duties, and picked up very quickly on the essence of how a car is constructed under the hood. Eventually, he was given an opportunity as a fill-in mechanic when one of the full-time mechanics was off for a month after sustaining multiple injuries in an automobile accident.

Isabella and Alfredo had been married for eleven years, and had two daughters by the names of Camila and Luciana. Isabella had tried relentlessly to convince Alfredo to return to school instead of working so many hours a day in a field with very little potential for advancement. Alfredo's hourly rate at Ignacio Security Firm was one dollar over the minimum wage, and because his wife's annual salary was significantly more than the salary he earned, Alfredo's pride, coupled with complacency, induced him to work more hours at his current job rather than adhering to his wife's sincere encouragement.

Isabella worked dayshift at St. Elizabeth Hospital as a Registered Nurse on the surgical recovery unit. She was an outstanding nurse, however, she had poor social skills when it came to relating to people. There were several nursing aides who worked under her authority, conducting tedious nursing tasks she felt were beneath her at this point in her career. She often talked down to these nursing aids who were subject to her authority, with the exception of those who shared her culture.

Every day after work, Isabella had the daunting task of helping both her daughters with their homework, and after their homework was completed, she usually would start preparing dinner for her family. Isabella's daughters would have been satisfied with only eating Kraft boxed macaroni and cheese, which they loved, but her husband expected a full course dinner meal when he came home from work. Alfredo generally worked the morning shift, but habitually he signed up for overtime shifts in the evening. His wife steadfastly tried to explain to him that she needed his help more at home with their daughters.

Isabella wanted Alfredo to work fewer hours either to become more involved with raising their children and their extracurricular school activities or to make the sacrifice to return to school himself. For Isabella, the overtime that made her husband absent from home just did not offer enough benefits for her to continue to be overwhelmed this way. Every time Isabella expressed her feelings about this to Alfredo, her husband would become irate and feel the need to defend his position as a husband. These disagreements led to Alfredo referring to his wife as an inadequate mother. Isabella desperately tried to prove to Alfredo—and even to herself—that she was in fact a good mother, but instead it seemed to minimize her voice concerning their lives.

Isabella turned the television on in the kitchen to watch Telemundo Chicago News while she prepared the cheesy beef empanadas Alfredo had told her he wanted for dinner. It wasn't long before she was yawning, and she found herself dozing off while she was dicing onions and garlic for her dish. After taking her daughter Camila to volleyball practice the previous day, she still had to complete the normal routine of her daily tasks after practice, so Isabella was already more than overextended today. But Isabella was looking forward to this weekend because she was off work. Unfortunately, today was only Wednesday. To make matters worse, Alfredo informed Isabella after climaxing from what he considered passionate lovemaking that he'd signed up to work extra shifts this weekend. Isabella felt nearly debilitated just thinking about the activities her daughters would want to do, all without Alfredo being a part of what once had been labeled as family time. Somehow, the lovemaking that had been the best thing about their marriage had become another chore as well. Just thinking about all of this was making her even more exhausted. Isabella just wanted to make it through the evening and get to bed as soon as possible.

But first she had to finish cooking dinner, fold the laundry from yesterday, and, lastly, wash Luciana's long hair that had become a tangled mess from rolling in the dirt on the baseball field while playing softball. Thinking about all of these chores while she was already weary and irritated. Isabella began to purposely cut the onions and garlic in larger chunks. Alfredo was a stickler about food enhancements such as bell peppers, garlic, and onions being cut very fine, which of course took even more of Isabella's time.

Isabella heard the front door of their house slam, and she ran to the living room, thinking one or both of her daughters were leaving the house without permission. When she made it to the living room, she could clearly see it was just Alfredo.

"What are you doing home? I thought you were working until midnight again," Isabella asked.

"I thought I was too, but they sent me home because this new black guy wanted to work, and they said I already have four overtime days this pay period," Alfredo said angrily.

Luciana heard what her father said and interrupted as she came into the living room. "My teacher said it's not right to describe people by a color the way we identify cars and clothes dad. We're supposed to say African Americans," Luciana explained. Alfredo ignored his daughter and pulled her closer to kiss her three times on the top of her forehead as she playfully struggled to get loose.

"Is that anyway to greet your father when he comes home after a hard day of work to spend quality time with his family? Say hello to your father the proper way." Isabella stood by, listening to the superficial interaction Alfredo was having with his daughter. She knew his declaration of "quality time" was simply based on the cancellation of his overtime shift.

"Hello, Papa, so what are we going to do tonight?" Luciana asked with anticipation. "Why don't we wait until your mother is done cooking dinner and has finished her chores, then maybe we could all play pass the sombrero. Tell your sister to come speak to her papaito. I'm going to watch some soccer on television until dinner is ready."

Excited that her father was home and they'd be playing pass the sombrero after dinner, Luciana scurried off to find her sister.

"If I were you, I would stop kissing your precious little conejito on the top of her head. I have to wash her hair of all the dirt she picked up from playing on the field," Isabella explained.

"Why didn't you wash it when you first got home from work? My little conejito wouldn't have soiled hair if her mother wasn't absent."

Infuriated by the audacity of Alfredo's comment, Isabella passive-aggressively shot back, "Since you have the time to abide in our la casa today, why don't you play the game with our daughters without me so I can finish dinner and other chores?" Alfredo didn't like this idea, because it would keep him from getting in front of the television to watch soccer. Plus, he felt Isabella was being sarcastic with him.

"What madre wouldn't want to spend time with her chamacas? Finish up with dinner, and let's have some valuable time as a familia," Alfredo said with authority. He then proceeded to the family room to watch soccer.

Isabella re-entered the kitchen to continue preparing dinner. By this time, her anger was mixed with feelings of inadequacy. She couldn't continue to cut her garlic and onions, because her hands were shaking profusely. After some time had passed and her hands leveled off from shaking, Isabella purposely chopped the onions and garlic in even bigger chunks than before. She wasn't just peeved at the way Alfredo had spoken to her while being totally inconsiderate of her feelings, she was also angry at herself for not confronting her husband's dismissive behavior towards her.

Isabella had grown up having a poor opinion of her mother, Rafaella, whom she considered as being weak for allowing mistreatment by her father, Macario, to continue. Isabella recalled a time when her mother hadn't precisely timed her husband's arrival home from work well. Her father had demanded that his warm bath be ready, and a hot meal after his bath with a cold beer. He'd conditioned Rafaella into believing their evening would go well if she did these things as he'd asked. Nevertheless, their evening was often maligned with yelling, including profanity toward her mother. However, on that night Isabella and her sister Natalia were eyewitnesses to their father's domestic abuse toward their mother.

Macario exited the bathroom wearing his hand-stitched robe designed and made by Rafaella. Macario consumed two forks full of the chicken linguine his wife had cooked. She stood across from her husband waiting for his approval. Macario nodded to his wife to let her know the dish was acceptable. When he was done chewing and swallowing his food, he reached for his beer can and said, "It's good. After one hundred failed experiments, you finally cooked it the way my mamito makes it."

He then took a big gulp from his beer can, but then stood up and spat all of the beer on his wife. Isabella and her sister Natalia were dumbstruck by what they were seeing. "I work twelve hours a day," he yelled, "and I have to come home to a warm can of piss. Let's see if you enjoy drinking hot urine." Macario grabbed Rafaella by her long ponytail and dragged her to the floor, with no regard for his daughters. He opened his robe and urinated on his wife while she repeatedly screamed that she was sorry. "Lo siento, Lo siento. Por favor, Lo siento."

Macario ignored Rafaella's apologies and pleas, and when he finished emptying his bladder, he dragged her to the icebox by her hair. "Get me an ice-cold beer before I detach every strand of El Pelo from your head." Rafaella screamed with excruciating pain, but she realized her husband would have no mercy. She desperately lunged to grab a beer from the bottom of the icebox. It was on that day that Isabella determined that her mother was inferior to her father, and she made herself a promise that she wouldn't mirror her mother's life.

By the time Isabella had completed all the preparations for the cheesy beef empanadas, she'd replayed the entire traumatic event in her mind. She placed two large baking sheets inside the stove prior to preheating the oven. It would be about six to ten minutes before she would have to drain the fat from the cooked beef, so she called Luciana to the kitchen and washed her hair in the sink to save time while cooking. After Isabella served her family dinner, she went to her and Alfredo's bathroom to shower. After her shower, she set out the nursing scrubs that she planned to wear to work in the morning, and she went to bed.

The next morning, she woke up to the earsplitting sound of the radio station on her alarm clock. The deafening sound woke up Alfredo as well, and he was not at all pleased by it. "Can you turn that damn radio down? Why do you have to turn it up so loud when others are still sleeping?" Alfredo yelled, making as much noise as the clock radio.

"I'm a heavy sleeper," Isabella responded, "and I have to get up on time to get the girls ready before I go to work. I didn't know you were off this morning."

"I'm not off, but waking up to salsa music blaring in my ear is not how I want to start my day." Isabella ignored Alfredo. His rationale for complaining this morning was not genuine enough for her to have empathy, since he would be getting up to work as well. Isabella was repelled by the idea that Alfredo would be getting up with her while she had to rush around getting her daughters ready for school so she could make it to work on time. When Alfredo would get up with the rest of the household, he expected a cooked breakfast and brewed hot coffee, and she'd already made up her mind that today was the day she would take a stance against his self-regarding expectations.

"I need to urinate before you get into the bathroom and hog all the hot water, and by the way, you left the pans on the stove and dishes in the sink. Not to mention the girls and I had to play pass the sombrero with just the three of us. I told them their mamito valued sleep more than time with her family." Alfredo turned to walk toward the bathroom, but Isabella decided to refute his accusation.

"What do you mean I left the dishes in the sink and on the stove? Those are your conejitos as well. What is wrong with you taking care of them and spending time with them? I do it all the time when you're working."

Alfredo turned and walked toward Isabella and leaned in to her so the point of his nose touched her nose. "Don't get sassy with me. You better know your place with me. You will not speak to me the way those colored women talk to their el hombre. At work you are the boss, but in this house, I am the big EL Jefe." Alfredo stood in front of her, staring to intimidate her. It was obvious she was afraid, and she opted to hold her tongue.

When Alfredo walked away to the bathroom, Isabella cried, because her husband had postured over her as though he would become physical with her. Isabella began to shake, which usually happened when she was frightened or distressed. She gathered herself, and grabbed her work scrubs off the hanger on the doorknob. She showered and dressed in the other bathroom that her daughters used. Then she helped Camila, and Luciana conclude their preparations. The three left the house without telling Alfredo they were leaving. Isabella drove her daughters to the Original House of Pancakes to have breakfast before driving them to school.

Alfredo was infuriated that he had to eat a bagel and drink orange juice for breakfast before going to work. He always told his wife he didn't trust coffee shops to make his coffee, but today he would have to do just that if he would be drinking any coffee at all. As he drove his usual route to work, there was a traffic jam on Michigan Avenue. Alfredo was very impatient, and due to the fact he was already boiling mad with Isabella after last night and her early-morning departure, he was now beside himself with anger. Plus, the stand-still traffic was going to make him late relieving the security guard who worked the overnight shift at the construction site. Even as a child, Alfredo had been very impatient, and over the course of his life, the decisions he made and actions he took when he couldn't be patient tended to have consequences.

Alfredo's parents had migrated to the United States from Chiapas, Mexico, when he was thirteen years old. Alfredo's father, Roberto, worked at a bar-restaurant there called Maria Cocina de Barrio, and when Alfredo was out of school on the weekends, he would accompany his father to work to earn money while the restaurant was at its busiest. Roberto was a food preparer and a dishwasher. He'd worked at the restaurant for minimum wage for seven years, but because he could dice food quickly for the cook , the chef would give him tips and bonuses because the preparing line was always stocked and the dishes were always clean. Alfredo was instructed not to take more than five plates at a time to the wash bin, and his job was to sweep the floors after his father had sliced fat from meat, peeled vegetables, and cut up garlic, tomatoes, onions, and peppers.

On one particular Saturday, the restaurant was filled to capacity, and there were people waiting outside for tables. The dishes were coming so fast to the kitchen that even at Roberto's top-notch speed of slicing and dicing, it was difficult for him to keep up with the pace of the orders that were coming to the kitchen. Roberto also had a severe case of gout, the joint in his left foot inflamed and swollen because of his increased uric acid levels from drinking an abundance of tequila the previous night. His hands moved as fast as ever on the preparation line, but he was slow in moving when he had to walk over from the preparation table back to the basin washing bin for the dishes. He yelled at Alfredo and asked him to do more than he normally would. It was only because the chef and the owner saw value in Roberto that he was allowed to have his son in the kitchen working. Other servers and food preparers were begrudging of the preferential treatment that was shown to Roberto and his son.

Now as soon as Alfredo returned to the kitchen with used dishes from now-vacant tables in the dining room, his father was asking him to wash dishes, which normally he would never do. Alfredo went back and forth from the dining area to the kitchen, bringing in plates, discarding leftover food, and washing the dishes. By the time he made it back to the dining area, a large party had just left after having dinner at three tables pushed together. Alfredo felt it was a waste of time to continuously run back and forth to the kitchen when he could carry more plates. He piled up nine plates at one time and was off to the kitchen, but because the plates were stacked so high, he couldn't see where he was stepping. After a customer dropped a tortilla shell with beef and salsa on it, Alfredo lost his footing, falling face first into the door to the kitchen, injuring himself and breaking all of the dishes.

The scene drew attention from a great many customers, and the owner apologized and told a particular group there would be no charge for their meal. When the owner went into the kitchen to confront Roberto about his son's accident, he could see Roberto was in no condition to work with his limited mobility in his lower extremities. He fired Roberto and told him and Alfredo to leave his restaurant now, and never to come back. With Chiapas already being one of the poorest cities in the thirty-two federal entities in Mexico, within two weeks Roberto and his family were living in desolate conditions. It was at that time Roberto seized the opportunity to bring his family to the United States. From that day forward, Roberto was extremely hostile toward Alfredo, and his wife was included in his fits of rage whenever she would intervene in the way he handled their son.

Alfredo texted his wife from his cell phone to let her know that what he believed to be a growing propensity for opting out of being a wife and mother, as she had done over the past couple of days, would not be tolerated. Isabella read the text but did not respond, and this maddened Alfredo even more.

She'd shared with her daughters over breakfast that she had opted not to play pass the sombrero with them last night because she was fatigued. She explained that because their father had been home, she'd taken advantage of the opportunity to get some much-needed rest. Isabella drove her daughters safely to school, and while sitting in the parking lot of her place of employment, she transformed her mentality from that of a subservient wife to that of the administrative nurse in charge of the forty-two-bed unit in the surgical recovery department. She entered the building with her stone-faced look and demeanor. She flashed her hospital I.D. badge to security officer Bell, whom she passed every morning. Isabella never looked directly at officer Bell to make eye contact, and she never spoke to officer Dorothy Brigham either. She walked onto the elevator, and just before the elevators closed, Dr. Nakkor stuck his arm between the elevator doors, and the doors reopened for him and three other residents to enter.

"Good morning, Dr. Nakkor. How are you this morning?" Isabella asked jovially. "Don't hold it against me if I don't share your sentiments," he said in a serious tone. "I'm on my way to your department to make rounds with my residents. I hear there was an admission last night, and somehow you guys ignored my order for this patient to have an x-ray on her hand."

"I'm just making it to work," Isabella explained. "Allow me to receive report from the overnight team, and if you would be so kind as to see that patient last, I'll have more pertinent information for you at that time."

"Please see that you do," Dr. Nakkor said.

Isabella quickly answered, "Yes, I'll get right on it, sir."

They exited the elevator and entered the unit. Isabella placed her jacket on the back of one of the computer chairs and placed her bag on the seat of the chair next to it.

She then proceeded directly to the report room, even though report was scheduled to begin at eight o'clock, and it was currently ten minutes before eight. When she sat at the head of the report table, she saw three books stacked on top of each other. She opened the book on top, searching for the name of the owner of the books. One of the nurses, Denise, entered the report room, followed by Connie, one of the nursing aides.

"Are these your books, Connie?" Isabella asked.

"No those aren't mine. I think those belong to Olivia," Connie answered immediately.

"Where is Olivia?" By the sound of Isabella's voice, Denise knew there was going to be trouble.

"I heard her say she was going down to the cafeteria to get some breakfast since reporting wasn't on time," Denise answered.

Isabella sighed heavily and shook her head in irritation.

"Good morning," Carol, one of the dayshift nurses, said as she entered the report room with Lolita, another dayshift nurse.

"Good morning, Carol. At least I hope it's a good morning," Isabella said.

"Why aren't there any assignment sheets available?" Lolita asked, setting her magazines and cup of coffee on the table. "I need to get my mind around where I'm working, and which patients I'm assigned to. I had Leslie in 326 yesterday, and her family was here almost the entire shift complaining about everything and questioning the doctor's orders. They behave as though they have great concern for her wellbeing, yet they smuggled in chocolate donuts and cheese danishes for her, knowing she's diabetic."

"Fidel went to make copies of the assignment sheets. He'll be in to give us report shortly," Isabella said, and then looking at the cover of one of Lolita's magazines: "Is that Sandra Echeverria the actress? She looks different."

Before Lolita could answer, Fidel the nightshift nurse entered the report room in dramatic fashion.

"It's so hard to get good help around here, I don't know where they find these people," he said as he swung his colorful scarf around his neck. Fidel's nursing scrubs were white with red peppermint stripes, and he habitually wore the white nurse's caps that nurses wore with their nursing uniforms in the fifties and sixties. He sat down to give report, flung his leg over his left kneecap as he leaned back in his chair to give report. "Well divas, we had an interesting and eventful night. My crew may as well work the day or evening shift, because we earned every bit of our pay overnight. We ran around so much tonight I was sweating, and you guys know I hate to sweat, due to the amount of hours it takes to make up this beautiful face." Carol laughed aloud at Fidel's attention-seeking antics.

The report room door swung open, and Nancy and Samantha entered the report room with Olivia following behind, balancing her breakfast tray and her coffee. Olivia sat down for report in front of her schoolbooks on the table while Nancy and Samantha stood against the wall. "What did we miss?" Samantha asked.

"You're right on time, divas. I'm just getting started," Fidel answered.

"Are those your books, Olivia?" Isabella asked.

"Yes, they're mine," Olivia said unassumingly.

"Why are your books on the report room table?" Isabella asked, with no regard for the present company.

"If you must know, they're books for my classes. On my lunch break I'm going to study for an exam I have tomorrow."

"She's in school, Isabella. Give her a break. We've all been there," Denise stated.

"I'm all for her going to nursing school. Why else would anyone be in this field and be limited to just a nursing assistant? I'm just trying to ensure our patients will be well cared for and not subject to neglect if her plan was to study when she should be working."

Everyone in the room was astounded by Isabella's presumption. Even her good friend Lolita deemed it unnecessary and excused herself from the reporting table and left the room.

"What I choose to do for a living shouldn't be a concern of yours. You've never seen me neglect any of our patients, and you never will. This feels very personal," Olivia said, prior to getting up from the table.

"You're working with me today, Olivia. I'll give you report on our patients after we make rounds," Carol said before she left the report room.

"If you kittens are done clawing the furniture, I can start my report so that I may go home to purr with my own feline," Fidel said, rolling his eyes.

Although Fidel's shift reporting was always animated, it was always accurate, and he left no stone unturned. When he'd given his report and was exiting the report room along with all the other nurses and nursing assistants, Isabella yelled out, "Oh, I ran into Dr. Nakkor outside the unit. He wanted to know why the new patient didn't have the X-Ray that was ordered by the admitting physician."

"Well, if Dr. Nakkor would've read Dr. Naansune's order correctly, he would've noticed there was no time frame on the order," Fidel said. "Why would I wake a patient that's resting comfortably to have them transported to another department? Our night was busy enough. I couldn't afford to have one of my nursing assistants off the floor for an extended period of time. Not to mention it takes transport more than an hour to get up here in the middle of the night whenever we request them. If Dr. Nakkor would spend more time thoroughly reading the orders of his colleagues, and less time wearing scrubs over his spandex underwear, he would be doing all of us a favor," Fidel continued with sarcasm.

"I'm not getting into that," Isabella responded in a passive aggressive manner. "Maybe you can explain it to him. He's making his rounds."

"I don't think so, mamacita. I am going home. I work the nightshift and not days for a reason. I've handled mine, now handle yours." Fidel spun around and walked away from Isabella in dramatic fashion. He didn't approve of the way Isabella had spoken to Olivia, and he sought to give Isabella the same level of attitude she had exhibited toward their colleague.

When Isabella exited the report room after penciling in her assignment schedule, she saw several nurses including Fidel gathered around Olivia at the end of the hall. Isabella assumed the gathering had to be about her and the way she had confronted Olivia openly in the report room. Isabella felt justified by the way she had handled the situation. She was convinced that she was simply advocating for the patients, and being the charge nurse, she rarely apologized for her actions or mistakes. The night shift crew began to disperse after noticing Isabella entering the nursing station.

Carol remained to give report on the patients they were assigned to, and after her report, she stated to Olivia, "Look, I know we're living in times where race seems to arise in most infractions. I personally think the majority of the time race is not the primary issue, but I can't help but feel like in this case it may be appropriate to see it that way. Prior to you entering the report room, Lolita came in with a bunch of magazines and set them on the report table, and not only did Isabella not question the purpose of the magazines, she asked Lolita about the woman that was on the front cover of the magazine. I like Isabella, don't get me wrong, but there are times it's very apparent she shows preferentialism to people of her own nationality."

"Believe me, it doesn't go unnoticed," Olivia said in a matter-of-fact manner. "That is something I deal with every day of my life. Nevertheless, this job is a means to an end until I'm finished with school. I just want to do my job, remain focused on my goals."

"You do an excellent job with our patients, Olivia. I enjoy working with you. I know when we're assigned the same patients, they will be well taken care of. You'll make a great nurse, because you already make my job easy," Carol said as she placed her hand on Olivia's shoulder. The phone rang at the nursing station, and Carol departed, thinking it might be the transport department responding to her page for transportation of her patient to the X-ray department.

The unit clerk yelled out after answering the phone, "Isabella, line three is for you."

Isabella picked up the phone, and it was her husband.

"I don't know what you're trying to prove, but don't you ever leave my house without letting me know where you're going."

"Alfredo, you leave our house most mornings without saying goodbye to our girls, and if you're not working overtime in the morning you sleep in, and do not even get up to see them off to school. So why is this morning any different?" Isabella genuinely inquired.

"You watch your tone and respect your husband, or do I have to impose my will to get your respect? Believe me, that's not what you want," Alfredo threatened his wife.

"I am at work, and I don't care to argue with you over the telephone," Isabella responded, then placed the receiver back on the telephone. The unit clerk, Antonella, who was within earshot of Isabella, could hear Alfredo yelling through the phone.

The phone rang again and Antonella answered. "St. Elizabeth Hospital, you've reached the Surgical Recovery Department. This is Antonella speaking, how may I help you?"

"Antonella, put my wife on the phone!" Alfredo shouted. Antonella took the receiver from her ear and stared at the phone as if though Alfredo could see her offended demeanor. She then turned to Isabella without saying a word.

"Is that my husband again?" Isabella asked, knowing the answer to her question. "Yes," Antonella answered with a serious tone.

"Please tell him I'm with a patient," Isabella instructed. Antonella was not happy about dealing with Isabella's personal issues, especially since she was now asking her to lie as well. She connected back to the line on hold and stated, "She's with a patient. Would you like to leave a message?"

"Yes, tell my wife to get to the phone or I'm coming up there," Alfredo demanded.

"I will give her the message sir," Antonella responded. "Look Isabella, I am not here to get into personal spats between you and your husband. The next time he calls, you'll have to take the call. I do not appreciate him yelling at me. I do not take that from my own amante, and I refuse to be subjected to that from your man." The phone began ringing again. "He also said if you do not get on the phone, he will be coming up here." Antonella then answered the phone in her usual professional manner. "St. Elizabeth Hospital, you've reached the Surgical Recovery Department. This is Antonella speaking, how may I assist you?"

In a more comforting tone Alfredo asked, "Can you put my wife on the phone, Antonella?"

Without missing a beat, Antonella responded, "Hold please, sir." Antonella looked over at Isabella. "It's for you."

Isabella was irritated that Antonella would not lie for her to avoid her husband. "Hello," Isabella answered.

"I don't think you want me to come up there. I don't give a rat's ass about you losing that damned job. You made a vow to be my wife, and you're indebted to be a mother to our daughters. You need to get back in line, or I will tear you apart and piece you back together again, do I make myself clear?"

Without hesitation Isabella answered to avoid unwanted consequences. "Yes, you've made yourself clear, and I will fall back in line."

Satisfied that Isabella's submission came without a rebuttal, Alfredo went on to say, "Good. I love you, and I will wake you when I make it home tonight so we can discuss this further."

Isabella answered, "Okay."

“I told you that I love you. You’re not going to say you love me back?”

Isabella surveyed her surroundings to see if anyone was paying attention. Her hopes were shattered, because all eyes were pierced in her direction, especially Antonella the unit clerk.

“Are you there?” Alfredo roared.

“Yes, I’m here. I love you too, Alfredo.” After Isabella answered her husband, several of the nurses and nursing assistants exited the nursing station, murmuring to one another. Her friend Lolita was seen simply shaking her head. Isabella ended the call, and placed the receiver back on the phone base. She was extremely embarrassed, but her embarrassment wasn’t enough to deter her from her authoritative mentality. “I’m sure you guys have better things to do besides stare at me. We have three admissions coming this morning, and I only see one admission packet in the bin. I suggest you began putting together admission packets before my admissions arrive,” Isabella stated, now talking directly to Antonella, trying to invoke fear into the other staff members who had just witnessed her consent to indignity.

Olivia exited the staff bathroom that was near the nursing station, and Isabella seized the opportunity to display her power once again. “I know you cannot be on a break already, when the shift just began. Did the orange juice from your breakfast travel through you that quickly? Have you even checked on your patients yet?”

Shocked that Isabella was targeting her once again in the presence of the treatment team and a few patients who were now awake, Olivia said, “Of course I’ve checked on my patients. I’ve taken the vitals of all the patients on this unit, including patients I wasn’t assigned to.”

"Thank you, Olivia, I really appreciate it," Nancy chimed in.

"Nevertheless, it's still too early for you to take unauthorized breaks," Isabella continued with her unreasonable stance.

"Look Isabella, I don't know what's your problem with me. I do my work, and no one else seems to have a problem with my work ethic except you. I'm starting to feel like your attacks are racially motivated because I'm African American, and if we have to take this to Human Resources, I will proceed with that."

Before Isabella could refute Olivia's charge, Dr. Nakkor yelled from down the hall as he and his team of residents hurriedly moved toward the nursing station. "I have to go downstairs and make my rounds on the pediatric floor. You asked me to see the newly admitted patient last, and that you would have information for me. Now tell me why she didn't go downstairs for an X-ray? Don't ever make me wait when I ask you to do something."

Once again, all eyes were on Isabella, and once again she submitted to authority when she was confronted. "The nightshift nurse reported there was no time stamp on the order written from the admitting doctor. I viewed the order myself, and confirmed that to be true. Not to mention you just stated that you wanted an X-ray but the order is for an MRI. I have paged transportation, and they are on their way as we speak," Isabella explained further.

"You see to it when I come back this afternoon to see my patient that I have something from Radiology I could use," Dr. Nakkor said firmly, and walked away.

Olivia never moved from standing in front of the restroom as she observed the entire exchange between Isabella and Dr. Nakkor. She stood there gazing at Isabella, and waited until she made eye contact with her. "I guess I have to be male with lighter pigmentation to get some respect around here, huh?"

THE ISSUE OF *Disconnect*

CHAPTER 2

CLARENCE SAT IN THE parking lot at Kingdom Grocery Store waiting on his wife, Gladys, who was picking up last-minute items for the backyard event they were having later this evening at their home. It was a warm June afternoon, and the sun was shining brightly. Nonetheless, there was a pleasant breeze that came through the windows of Clarence's Lincoln Navigator. Clarence enjoyed the breeze as he laid his head back on the headrest, thinking about how he would enjoy the week of vacation he had just embarked upon. Clarence planned to retire next year from his job as an engineer for High-rise 500 in downtown Chicago. His wife had already been retired from One Day Recovery as a substance abuse counselor for more than three years. Gladys and Clarence usually had a minimum of three outdoor events during the warm months of the year. They particularly enjoyed entertaining guests, and usually their events consisted of twenty to twenty-five people, ranging from the ages of forty-five to sixty.

Clarence and Gladys had three adult children. Their middle child, Rosalyn, was twenty-two years of age and had just recently graduated from Howard University. Rosalyn made the surprising decision to remain in Washington, D.C., to live when she was offered a position at the Department of Health and Human Services. When Rosalyn left home for college after graduating from high school, Clarence and Gladys decided they would host more mature backyard events after years of having family parties to accommodate their children and the children of their guests as well. Clarence couldn't wait to try out his new combo grill, which had the ability to both smoke and grill food.

His quiet moment and pleasurable thoughts were interrupted by the loud music that drowned out the smooth jazz he was listening to in his truck. Clarence looked over, and the car with the deafening noise playing vulgar music was pulling into the space next to him.

He smelled marijuana, and after the four young men who were accompanied by a strikingly beautiful young lady parked and turned off the music, their voices were just as loud as the music they were blaring in their vehicle. The look on Clarence's face told the entire story about how he felt about what he was witnessing.

"Terrence, why that old dude mean-mugging you like he want to throw some hands with you," a young man by the name of Marquise said, sparking others to laugh. "I don't know why he's staring so hard, unless he wants to buy some weed from us or some booty from Keisha. If not, he might want to mind his old-ass business."

Clarence didn't respond, but he didn't refrain from his disapproving gaze at the young men, either. Clarence heard knocking against his rear window, and when he turned around, it was his wife with the groceries by the trunk of his car. He immediately exited his vehicle and told his wife to get into the truck so he could load the groceries.

Subsequently, after Clarence loaded the groceries and pushed the cart into the cart corral, he re-entered his vehicle somewhat disturbed by his interactions with the young, discourteous group of individuals. He did not want his wife to know what had taken place, because typically Gladys would blow the incident way out of proportion, and try to fix it without full understanding of the situation.

"Did you invite Charles to the barbecue?" Gladys asked.

"Yes, I invited him. He's my friend. Why wouldn't I invite him?" Clarence responded, knowing Gladys's question was all-out loaded.

"Well, Katherine is *my* friend, and just because they're separated, I don't see why she should be excluded from our annual event. Why does Charles get to come, and she doesn't?" Gladys probed.

"He gets to come because I invited him. Did you invite your friend Katherine, since you have all this great concern? Look, I'm not about to have a squabble with you about Katherine and Charles. They decided to separate, which doesn't have anything to do with you and I. That's their problem, their decision. Please don't make their drama ours. I invited Charles the way I always do, and you're welcome to invite Katherine. I don't have a problem with Katherine. What happened between them is between them," Clarence explained.

"Do you know if he's coming by himself? I don't want to invite Katherine into an awkward position," Gladys asked in a more appropriate tone.

"We didn't have that discussion, Gladys. I didn't ask him. At the time I didn't feel the need to. I think you should invite Katherine and let them deal with their own issues. Katherine is our friend the way Charles is our friend. We don't want to be in the position where we invited one and not the other, because that would look like we were choosing sides."

"You're right," Gladys said. "I'm going to call Katherine right now and invite her if she doesn't already have plans."

Clarence felt the need to explain his underlying principle further. "I totally understand your feelings about Katherine, but once again, let's not let their issues become our issue. They were our friends before their split. It would be wise to invite them both to eliminate any form of exclusion and hurt feelings. Who knows, it may be possible that they could work things out and find their way back to one other," Clarence said.

"I doubt that very seriously, but you're right about letting them handle their own affairs," Gladys replied.

"I'm also right about that sound from you I haven't heard in a while with the assistance of my new friend the blue pill," Clarence added.

Gladys smiled but offered no response.

"How about we let the rest of the day be great, the way it started out this morning," Clarence said, before putting his truck in gear and pulling out.

Gladys continued smiling at Clarence's reference to that morning's activity.

She had been satisfied that morning in a way she thought was no longer possible. Gladys loved her husband, and sex was far from being high on their priority list at this stage of their lives, but she still desired to physically connect with her husband on occasion.

"I didn't realize it's one o'clock already. We have to get home. Percy is coming over to help me grill some of the meat before our guests arrive. I prefer not to be stuck by the grill while entertaining our guests. He's bringing his grill so we can cook twice as fast, in half the time," Clarence continued.

"Why didn't you tell me Percy was coming over early?" Gladys asked worriedly. "I seasoned all of the meat last night, but our house is not suitable to be having guests just yet."

"Percy is family, and he's not focused on the status of our house. That's women's stuff. Besides, we'll be in the backyard on the deck."

Gladys wasn't satisfied with Clarence's justification for not cluing her in about Percy arriving prior to the event. Gladys had grown up in a household with a mother who had obsessive compulsive disorder, commonly known as OCD. Her mother, Mary, had insisted that everything in their household be organized and done by a certain time of the day. Her father, Melvin, did not adhere to his wife's obsessions, and he often kicked his shoes off at the door and threw other clothing and items wherever he saw fit in the house. Mary would quickly rush behind him to put these things in an order suitable for her.

However, Gladys and her brother, James, were forced to adopt their mother's way of life. Their beds had to be made a certain way, and the bed had to be facing toward the east side of the house. When Gladys and James would enter the house, they would have to remove their shoes, and their shoelaces would have to be either tied or tucked inside of the shoes. Gladys would never bring any of her friends to their home. She would always go and visit her friends at their houses.

When she was seventeen years of age, she was finally given permission by her father to date, with the condition that the boy she dated had to come to the house, so that Melvin could meet him. Without her father knowing, Gladys went out on a couple of dates with a boy name Dennis, but in order for her to go skating with Dennis and his family one particular Saturday evening, she knew Dennis would have to come to her house to be interrogated by her father, which would surely embarrass her. The night before Dennis was scheduled to come meet her father before they would go skating. Gladys cleaned the house from top to bottom, knowing this was always the expectation of her mother before company was allowed in the house. She waited until Saturday afternoon, however, to mop the floors in the house so that the floors would meet her mother's standard of approval prior to Dennis's arrival. After Gladys mopped the floors, she walked over to Dennis's house to again forewarn him of what the meeting with her father would entail.

Gladys was sure she'd done everything to minimize Mary's fixations about visitors entering their home when the home was not suitable for company. When Dennis entered their home with Gladys, she walked him into the den, where her father spent a lot of time alone and apart from the family. Once she had introduced Dennis, her father asked her to leave the room.

"Dad, can I stay? I promise not to interrupt," Gladys pleaded.

"No, I think you should go change your clothes. I'm looking at that outfit you have on. I wouldn't deem it to be appropriate to be going skating with this boy and his family."

When Gladys walked out of the den to go to her room to change into different clothing, her mother was in the kitchen feverishly washing plates and glasses from the china set that was kept in the cabinets above the sink. "You have the audacity to have this boy in my house with these filthy plates in the cabinet. How dare you embarrass me this way?"

Gladys was stunned by her mother's words. She'd worked very hard to organize and clean the house to avoid this kind of engagement. "Mom, I didn't wash the plates in the cabinet because they were already washed before we put them in the cabinet the last time. Besides, Dennis is not going to look in our cabinets. We're leaving as soon as Dad talks to him and I've changed my clothes."

Mary was enraged and unceasingly hit Gladys with a wet dish towel to display her anger. Gladys yelled profusely, and it took her father and Dennis to pull Mary away from striking Gladys further. This incident profoundly traumatized Gladys. She did not go skating with Dennis that evening, and her relationship with her mother took a turn for the worse from that day forward. As Gladys evolved into an adult, she began to unconsciously display traits of obsession to clean the way her mother had imposed upon her. However, she never was clinically diagnosed with OCD or displayed the same severity of compulsions as her mother.

There had been times in their marriage when Clarence would directly remind Gladys that she was exhibiting fixations similar to her mother, and this was one of those times.

"It just would've been nice if you would have communicated that Percy was coming by early. Our house is a great representation of us, and I just want to make it presentable no matter who comes by."

Clarence knew Gladys could be sensitive and defensive when the time came to acknowledge her overindulgent ways of organizing. But after twenty-one years of marriage, Clarence knew when to press and when to retreat, so for the sake of argument he simply responded, "Okay baby, you're right."

Within twelve minutes, Clarence had made it to their home. His timing was perfect, as he saw Percy pulling up on the other side of the street with his barrel grill tied down to the back of his Chevy Silverado pickup truck. Clarence assisted Percy with carrying the grill through the garage and into his backyard before gathering the items Gladys had purchased for the event. This was strategic by Clarence to eliminate any reasons for Percy to enter their home. Percy simply waved to Gladys before taking the grill from his rear cab.

Clarence took a while before he came back out of the house after taking the groceries inside. When he entered the yard from the house, he noticed that Percy had already ignited the coals on both grills. "I know you didn't put your hands on another man's brand-new grill before he had the chance to break it in himself. This has to be one of the thy shall not commandments somewhere in the Bible," Clarence said jokingly.

"Look man, you asked me to come help you cook this meat so you can enjoy your guests instead of being glued to this grill. If you have all these unwritten rules that need to be followed, barbecue the meat by yourself, and I will see you at six o'clock when everyone else gets here," Percy said, just as jokingly.

Clarence and Percy had known each other since they were teenagers at Edward Tilden High School. They became good friends when they made the school's football team together. Percy was always outspoken, so his direct deflection of Clarence's comment about orientating his barbecue grill was a typical response from him.

When they were in high school, Percy protected Clarence from some bullies who were part of a gang trying to recruit Clarence by intimidation. Percy was already on the Varsity Football team from the previous year as a freshman, and most of his friends were also his football teammates, along with guys on the wrestling team. Percy wrestled for the school in the off-season from football, and one day he was re-entering the school through a side door after leaving school grounds for lunch, which was not permitted. He witnessed some of the school's tough guys who were gang-affiliated pressing Clarence against his locker while threatening him, and giving him limited options, particularly not in his favor, to join their Black P Stone organization.

Percy saw what was happening, but he continued up the flight of stairs to attend the biology class he was already late for. The guys who were part of a gang didn't mess with Percy, because he was tall in stature and also had the backing of both the football team and the wrestling team. Clarence was above average in height, but he weighed about two hundred and forty pounds. He was clinically an overweight kid, but he was a solid kid who obviously didn't know his own strength.

After Percy's biology class was over, he was standing in the hall talking to a girl named Brandy who was in his second-period English class. Percy did not attend class that morning, but Brandy always kept him abreast of what was going on in class. His teacher, Mr. Smith, gave him leeway and preferentialism because playing middle linebacker, Percy was one of the school's football stars.

Once again Percy took notice of two guys who were Blackstones badgering Clarence, but this time when Clarence was pushed by one of the guys, he exploded with anger and rammed the guy against a locker with force, and he picked the other gang member up and slammed him down to the floor. Percy took immediate notice and walked over to take control of a situation that Clarence already appeared to have under control.

"Hey, y'all, let it be known, this is my cousin and he is not to be messed with," Percy announced while everyone on the third floor paid close attention. Clarence was so unsure of himself, he hadn't a clue to the brute strength he possessed. Clarence viewed Percy's intervention as much-needed protection. What he didn't know was that after Percy saw the way Clarence had handled himself, he set out to coerce him to join the football team, to be a part of an untouchable group in the school, and they had been friends ever since that time.

"Hey man, did you invite Charles to your event? I know Katherine's probably going to be here as well, right?" Percy asked.

"Yes, I invited him. Actually, Gladys and I were just discussing them in the car on the way home. My wife just invited Katherine today. We were in a no-win situation. If we decided to invite one of them and not invite the other, that would make us look like we chose a side and iced the other one out. So, we decided to invite them both and let them work out their own issues, even though it's going to be awkward as hell," Clarence explained.

"Man, when all those women get together and start drinking those fruity drinks, it's going to be attack season at some point tonight. It won't even matter whose fault it is that they've separated. My wife was asking me about it earlier. I simply said, 'Deneice, Clarence and Gladys invited us. I am not in charge of the guest list, and I didn't ask about it.' Clarence, I've been married to my wife long enough to know that was a loaded question. They are going to hornswoggle that brother tonight. You just watch what I tell you. He's my guy and all, but I like peace in my house more than I like Charles. So, I'm staying neutral to all those hypothetical questions they ask."

Clarence nodded his head in agreement with Percy, while laughing at his justification. "I just hope he gets here early before Katherine does. The last thing he wants to do is walk into the event late, and walk past all those ladies after they've had a couple of margaritas and are in rare form with woman support mode," Clarence said.

"I hear you. I feel for him, but I can't save him on this one. If I say anything, Deneice will automatically think I'm cosigning on Charles leaving Katherine. I like my wife's cooking, I like the sex we have, and I can't stand chaos in my home, so I'm staying out of it," Percy said.

Charles and Percy were finally done smoking and grilling all of the food in about three-and-a-half hours. Percy went home to shower and to pick up his wife so they could come back to the event on time.

When they did, Deneice entered the patio with a large pan of her famous three-cheese lasagna. Gladys stood up to greet her as she walked toward the few guests who had already arrived. "Hey girlfriend, how you doing?" Gladys said as she embraced Deneice, and took the pan out of her hand. "I told you, you didn't have to bring anything. I cooked more than enough side dishes, and I hired a caterer who attends my church for more side dishes. She already made two full pans of her Swedish meatballs for me."

Deneice heard what Gladys was trying to explain, but it had been engrained in her from her mother at an early age never to show up for any event empty-handed.

"Hello, sexy lady, you're wearing that black dress, and you act like you can't call anyone. You must've been a bad girl. Seems like Percy won't let you out of the house anymore," Ramona said as she came over to hug Deneice.

"My number hasn't changed, and I know you must have me mixed up with Stephanie. I've been married too long to Percy to play those kinds of games. Percy doesn't even have that kind of authority," Deneice said with all seriousness.

"Look at her coming into the party slinging shade already," Stephanie said, sitting in one of the patio chairs. "I didn't have anything to do with what you and Ramona were talking about. How did my name get in that conversation?"

"Whatever, girl, stop being so sensitive," Deneice said as she leaned down to give Stephanie a hug.

"Ladies, I'll be back after I put the lasagna in the kitchen, and I'm going to mix up some margaritas for everyone," Gladys announced, receiving some applause and encouragement from the women.

"I've been married for twenty-three years, and I still don't understand these men. Every year Gladys and Clarence throw at least three events during the warm months, and all of our husbands make a beeline straight for that garage," Stephanie said.

"I know, my husband wasn't even going to come speak to everyone before he headed for that garage. If I hadn't told him how rude that is, he would've continued directly back there," Marilyn said with irritation.

"Girl, let them stay out there in that garage looking at barbecue grills and tool boxes while they're discussing sports. I enjoy having stimulating conversation with my lovely sisters, who can obviously understand my plight as a woman and a mother. Besides, Gladys knows the perfect time to call the boys in from outside to brush their teeth and take a bath for the night," Monica said, and all of the women laughed at her sarcasm.

After they finished laughing, Katherine walked into the yard and headed toward the patio to join her friends. "I was hoping I was going to see you. How you holding up?" Stephanie asked Katherine.

"I'm doing just fine. How are you ladies doing?" Katherine replied with a perplexed look on her face.

"How are the kids, Katherine?" Ramona chimed in, feeling compelled to say something.

"Keith and Kamara are doing well, I guess. They're not exactly kids anymore, and I just allow them to live their own lives," Katherine explained. "Keith decided he was satisfied with just an associate degree, and now he's working at Amazon delivering packages while living with some girl that's two months pregnant by him. She doesn't work, she doesn't go to school, and she already has a two-year-old son by another man. Kamara finished school, and she is about to embark on a master's program for Human Resources Management in August. She consistently reminds me that she's an adult and not a child anymore, but every time she has a shortfall in her finances, I'm always her first option for financial support."

"That's all of them. They're so quick to tell you they are adults, but the moment life throws them a curveball, they're so comfortable asking for money as though they were still kids," Monica added.

"Well, at least all of your children are out of the house. I have a sixteen-year-old who think she's twenty-five and an eighteen-year-old who thinks we're supposed to pay her college tuition, but feels she is absolved from any household chores. I asked her does she think her father and I are supposed to provide for her, be her maid and butler too, in our very own home at this stage of her life?" Ramona said.

The women's attention was stolen after hearing loud, profanity-laced music that drowned out the soft ballads of rhythm and blues they were listening to. The music suddenly stopped, and Clarence and Gladys's youngest daughter came through the gate and maneuvered her way up the walkway onto the deck of the patio where the women were sitting.

"Hi ladies, I didn't know my parents were having a party tonight. I guess that means they're in for the night. Maybe we could use my mom's truck after all," Bridgett said while looking back at her two friends, Lexus and Keisha.

"Hi Bridgett, how've you been?" Deneice asked.

"I'm fine, Aunt Deneice. I'm sorry, where are my manners? Ladies, this is Keisha and Lexus, Lexus and Keisha, these are my aunts. This is my Aunt Deneice, this is my Aunt Ramona, this is my Aunt Monica, this is my Aunt Stephanie, and this is my Aunt Katherine. Auntie Katherine, tell Kamara to call me please. I lost my phone, and I don't have her phone number memorized," Bridgett rambled on.

"I hate to say it, but this technology is making your generation less intelligent. You are only using a small portion of your brains," Monica scolded.

Just then Gladys came out of the house and laid eyes on her daughter. "Hi Mom, you look lovely today. I didn't know you were having a party tonight." Gladys knew Bridgett had some sort of purpose, the way she complimented her.

"Hello, Bridgett, thank you. Now please explain to me why you're here," Gladys said in a calm manner.

"We're going to the Warehouse tonight, but Keisha's father wants his car back at nine o'clock. I came to ask you can I use your truck and bring it back to you in the morning?" Bridgett asked quickly.

"Absolutely not. I am entertaining, and I'd appreciate it if you brought the rest of the margaritas on the tray on the counter, and the remainder of it in the blender. Your father is in the garage. Maybe you can ask him if you could use his truck, because you're not getting mine."

Bridgett did not like the answer she received, and she had to let her mother know about it. "You want me to go in the house and do something for you, serve your guests, but you're not willing to let me use the ride?" All eyes focused on Bridgett at the same time. She was the only person who didn't recognize she'd crossed a line.

"Miss lady, you don't have to bring the margaritas out. I said no about my car, and that's what I mean. You have no problem holding your hand out for money, but now when I ask you to do something, I'm supposed to submit to you like you're the parent."

Before Bridgett could respond, Clarence came walking toward the deck from the garage. He saw his daughter and her friends, and the look on his face showed he was not enthusiastic about seeing them at this time. Clarence was always happy to see his daughter, but this event with his and Gladys's friends had been in the planning for weeks and something they all had looked forward to.

"Hi, Daddy," Bridgett said warmly to her father.

"Hey, baby," Clarence responded, while leaning over to kiss his daughter on the forehead. "Was that you guys playing that loud vulgar music?" Clarence asked.

Bridgett smiled but didn't respond. "You know better than that, Bridgett. What kind of young lady listens to that trash that simply degrades and disrespects women?"

"It's not my car, Daddy. I can't control what Keisha plays in her car. She gave me a ride here so I could come ask if I could use your car tonight."

Gladys shook her head and just watched to see if Bridgett's manipulation would work before she intervened.

"Aren't you the girl that was with those boys at the grocery store this afternoon? I remember one of those young punks you were with called you Keisha, just as my daughter said," Clarence asked sternly.

Keisha answered sheepishly, "Yes."

"Young lady, why were you in the car with those guys? They were playing the same kind of loud music you were just listening to. I take it you were smoking marijuana with them as well? Those young men indirectly threatened me, and hinted they would hurt me if I continued looking at them. Do you know they were auctioning you off like you were some prostitute?" The more Clarence talked, the more profoundly the facial expressions changed on the faces of their guests.

"They weren't auctioning me off, sir, they just talk stupid like that sometimes. I don't really pay them much attention. They're all talk and like to show off for one another."

Clarence stood in front of Keisha for a moment but didn't utter a word. Ramona turned down the music slightly, and everyone present was waiting to see what Clarence was about to say next.

Finally, he said, "Bridgett, go ask the men in the garage to come out to the deck. You young ladies go and have a seat up on the deck." Clarence motioned in the direction of the other women who were sitting on the deck. When Clarence finally looked around, he noticed Katherine, and he immediately greeted and hugged her. "I apologize, ladies. I know you didn't come here for this, but I can't allow this teaching moment to go by the wayside for my daughter and these young ladies."

"You do whatever you have to do, Clarence. I wish more of our men took charge instead of being so politically correct these days. I'm going to sit right here and nurse this margarita while you educate." Clarence smiled at Deneice's encouragement, but he was still seriously thinking how he wanted to approach this as the men began to sit next to their wives around the bench and in the open chairs on the deck.

Clarence finally decided he'd just tell the story of what had transpired earlier in the day and then utilize the wisdom from both the men and the women who were already present. He sat next to Gladys and grabbed her margarita out of her hand to help himself to a nice big gulp before he began to speak.

"I have an issue, and it's with your generation. You millennials and your thought processes scare the hell out of me. The older I get, I realize that soon your generation will be running this country. Truth be told, that frightens me to no end. Nevertheless, all of these men and women here tonight have an abundance of life experiences. I want you ladies to learn from them, especially the women, but I need help too from you guys. I saw this young lady today with these disrespectful poor excuses for men, and I have to admit, I have a strong dislike for this generation, because they have no honor or respect for anything and anyone.

Earlier today my wife and I went to the grocery store to pick up some last-minute things for this event, and I'm in my truck enjoying this beautiful spring day, listening to Ella Fitzgerald. All of a sudden, this repetitive heart-rending music drowns out the smooth grooves I'm listening to. I hear some boy talking fast while having a profanity-laced tirade over what it is they call music. I look over at the car that pulled up next to me, and it's a group of young men in one of those souped-up cars with big wheels on it. They pull next to me and finally silence the disturbing noise, but their voices are just as loud. The entire parking lot reeks of marijuana smoke. This beautiful young lady who sits before you is in the car with these young men. One of them says, 'Why that old dude staring at you so hard?' The other the kid responds, 'Unless he wants to buy some weed, or some booty from Keisha, he might want to mind his old-ass business.' I wasn't at all scared, because I'm licensed to conceal and carry. I always keep my piece in my armrest. I just continued to stare at how clueless and foolish they were. I didn't even tell my wife what happened, because she thinks I'm too hard on these clueless people and this disrespectful generation. So, I have a series of questions I need to ask tonight. I need feedback from all of you. But most importantly I need your help with giving direction to this new millennial generation that's here in your presence now," Charles said as he pointed in the direction of Bridgett and her friends.

It was at this point Bridgett realized her father and his middle-aged guests were about to inflict a back-in-my-day lecture upon them. "Dad, I just want to know if I could use your car. We're not about to sit here and take responsibility for all the things that are wrong with the world today," Bridgett stood up and said with a sense of entitlement.

But before Charles could address the rudeness of his daughter, Monica quickly intervened. "Sit down, Bridgett. There is clearly a reason that God gave you two ears and one mouth. You're proving what your father is saying by the way you're handling this right now. Today you're about to learn that being an adult is not just about doing what you want to do, but it's about doing what you have to do. Believe me, it's for the best."

Bridgett sat down reluctantly, now totally embarrassed in front of her friends. By the smiles on Charles and Gladys's faces, it was apparent they greatly approved of Monica's charge toward their daughter.

"Now what's your name again, young lady?" Monica asked Keisha while pointing in her direction, but her eyes were looking downward as she took a sip from her margarita.

"Oh me, my name is Keisha," she answered.

"Tell me, why did you think it was okay for you to be in a car full of young men?"

Keisha pondered Monica's question for a few seconds, then looked around at Lexus and Bridgett for support before finally answering. "What do you mean? Those are my guys. I've been knowing them from off the block all of my life." Deneice noticeably shook her head, indicating she didn't approve of Keisha's response.

"How many boys were in the car again?" Monica asked.

"Four. What difference does it make?" Keisha shot back with attitude this time. "First of all, don't get me misunderstood for one of your girlfriends," Monica said. "I am a fully grown woman, and I will be respected. I'm trying to teach you how to have some respect for yourself. Please don't get me confused with the person that's allowed you to exhibit this apparent fabrication of womanhood. Now, don't you know the moment you entered that vehicle with four boys, that immediately signified the lack of respect you have for yourself, and it also indicated the lack of respect these boys have for you as well? That's how they can play loud and vulgar music in your presence. Clarence said the music was tainted with profanity, and I'm positive it was humiliating to women. So, you're riding in the car with these boys and..."

"They are men. You continue to say boys," Keisha interrupted.

"I beg to differ," Deneice intervened.

"Okay, Keisha, for the sake of argument let's call them men, but that label will be determined shortly after I make my point," Monica stated to stay on task. "As I was saying, you're riding around in the car with these men, and they are smoking marijuana. Are they smoking the kind of marijuana that draws everyone's attention, that marijuana they call Loud?"

Keisha answered reluctantly, "I guess."

"Were you smoking marijuana with these men? Obviously at least one of these men was operating this vehicle while inhaling illegal substances." Gladys smiled and grunted, knowing Monica was about to go in for the kill.

"No, I don't smoke Loud, but weed ain't nothing. At least they're not using dope, crack or something like that," Keisha tried to justify.

"Aunt Monica, can I say something, please?" Bridgett asked. Monica turned to look at her, and by the way she glared at Bridgett, it was evident already how she felt about the intrusion before she answered. "No, you may not, but you will get your chance at some point. I'm sure your parents and everyone here wants to know what in the world you have in common with a friend that rides around in cars with men who disrespect women and smoke drugs."

Clarence didn't interrupt Monica's deposition, but the smile of approval he once had on his face had now turned into a frown after Monica raised a relevant point about Keisha being Bridgett's friend.

"I'm not trying to be disrespectful, but that's why my generation don't show a lot of respect to our elders. Y'all always trying to put us down, or talk down to us. Y'all act like we don't know anything. Just because y'all are older than us don't mean you know everything," Keisha stated bluntly. Bridgett shook her head, signifying to Keisha that she was treading on the edge.

"Did she just imply her elders don't deserve her respect, that she is their equal and deserves an equal amount of respect?" Gladys asked while sliding to the edge of her seat and setting her glass on the patio table.

"Uh oh, wrong time to take a stance. She has awakened Sister Souljah right now," Percy said.

"I'm sorry, Monica, I have to get in on this, because I can't believe the insolence of this girl's ill-mannered mindset. How old are you, honey?" Gladys asked with seriousness.

"I'm twenty-two," Keisha answered.

"You live with your parents, don't you?" Gladys asked.

Keisha surveyed the attentive stares at her before she answered. "I live with my mother, but I pay rent."

"Do you know how much your mother's rent or mortgage is?" Gladys probed further.

"I give her two hundred dollars a month and sometimes I buy food, so Mrs. Williamson, if you're suggesting I'm an adult that doesn't carry my own weight, I do," Keisha emphasized with absolute confidence.

Many of the adults centered around Keisha and her friends began to laugh. Their laughter was largely due to the fact that Keisha naively believed that her contributions to her mother's household were acceptable contributions.

"Please don't laugh, guys," Gladys continued. "I want her to really know in this city we live in, the going rate for a mortgage is between fourteen hundred to two thousand dollars. Keisha, that donation to your household couldn't include the utilities and the luxuries you've come accustomed to. Baby, I'm willing to bet the young men you were with today also live with their parents as well. If they aren't living with their parents, I'm sure they're living off someone else. I'm making this point because your age group are quick to point out that you are adults, independent, but in actuality you don't have a clue to what it means to be an adult that's able to stand on your own two feet with no help from anyone else. You cannot ask grown people for help, money, and even their cars yet still want to be viewed as equals to adults."

Bridgett knew her mother was referring to her when she made mention of the car. "Mom, with all due respect, I came here to ask could I borrow your car so I can go out with my friends tonight. We didn't stop by here for a lecture. We're adults too. I'm sure you made some mistakes too, Mom. You weren't always perfect," Bridgett said, trying to save face in front of her two friends.

"First, I'm going to educate you on that cliché you used, 'with all due respect.' You don't say 'with all due respect' right before you disrespect someone," Gladys said. "As far as whether I made mistakes in my imperfect life, I'm not the topic of discussion here. The moment you entered our party without an invitation or any kind of forewarning with your company of friends, you were subject to this kind of enlightenment. The problem with your generation is, you spend far too much time talking and wanting to be heard when you should be listening." A few of the ladies began snapping their fingers in unison, giving approval that Gladys's assessment was very accurate.

"No offense, ma'am, but the problem with your age group is you've disconnected yourselves from our generation, and you constantly put us down, and that's why we don't listen to anything you have to say," Keisha asserted.

"Point taken, but I don't think you can blame me or this small group of individuals at this event for your lack of respect, lack of intelligence, and your lack of common sense. No offense," Gladys shot back.

"Maybe there is a disconnect between generations," Clarence said. "I can honestly say I don't enjoy being around you millennials. That's exactly why you see no one presently invited to this event under the age of forty-five. I don't care to be around people that talk loudly whenever they do decide to communicate. Otherwise their faces are habitually glued to a phone screen. You millennials have nothing of substance to talk about. You can't blame our generation for that." When Clarence finished his statement, his attention was turned toward Charles and the woman who accompanied him as they walked from the inside of the garage and up the walkway toward the deck. Charles proudly held his date Audrey's hand as they walked briskly toward the deck.

"I just know he did not bring another woman here," Monica said with disgust. "Clarence, I know you live in the suburbs, but this is not the fifties and sixties. Your garage door is wide open. You have all kinds of things visible for unsavory characters," Charles stated.

Clarence didn't comment right off. He was absolutely stunned by what he was seeing. "Oh yeah, thanks. I intended to go back to the garage with the fellas but we got into a discussion about generational differences. Bridgett, go let the overhead door down in the garage for me, please," Clarence instructed.

"Hello everyone, this is Audrey, and Audrey this is everyone."

"Hello, everyone, you have a huge backyard, and I love your deck. I've always seen that most decks were painted, but I love how authentic your wood looks. Is that cedar wood or redwood?" Audrey asked Clarence.

"It's cedar wood and thank you. This is my wife Gladys. This is my friend Percy, and that's his wife Deneice. This is Monica, and this is her husband Reginald. This is Ramona, and this is her husband Kevin, and this is Larry and his wife Stephanie. Last but certainly not least, this is Katherine," Clarence said after everyone appeared to speak at the same time.

"Katherine, I didn't know you were going to be here. Can we be adults about this? I mean, we really have no reason to have any disagreements at this point," Charles explained.

"Gladys and Clarence, excuse me, but somebody has to put this ignoramus in his place," Deneice said. Percy shook his head, knowing the evening was about to take a turn for the worse, as he had predicted.

"Audrey, it's nice to meet you, and I'm sure under better circumstances things would be much different, but do you know this is Charles's wife Katherine? And how old are you, anyway?"

The men were cringing and murmuring amongst themselves, but the ladies all looked at Charles with piercing stares, not only because Charles had showed up accompanied by another woman, but with a woman who looked half his age.

"What's up, Audrey," Keisha said before Audrey could answer Deneice's question. "What's up, Keisha. I haven't seen you at the Warehouse lately," Audrey responded, opting to ignore Deneice's original question.

"We were about to turn up there now, but we stopped by here first and got caught up in a situation," Keisha said.

"Wait, you guys know each other?" Gladys asked with confusion.

"Yes, we went to the same high school, and my little brother dates her younger sister," Keisha continued to explain, feeling vindicated.

"I think it is so disrespectful that you would show up here knowing it was a possibility Katherine would be here. What the hell is wrong with you, Charles?" Deneice yelled.

"No, it's okay, we're separated now. He can see whomever he wants to see, and do whatever he wants to do," Katherine chimed in.

"No, it's not all right. This son of a bitch owes you more than that. You were married for twenty-four years and have children together. He owes more respect to you than that. Hell, he owes more respect to everyone here," Deneice said, seeking support.

"How about you mind your own business and focus on your own marriage?" Charles shot back.

"Hey man, watch how you talk to my wife," Percy said while rising from his chair.

"I guess us millennials aren't the only individuals that can be loud and disrespectful," Keisha said with a huge grin on her face.

THE ISSUE OF STATU$

CHAPTER 3

THE SMELL OF RAW grass permeated through Lawrence's bedroom, but he kept his eyes closed, trying not to take in any of the sunlight that was shining through his bedroom window. The smell of the grass became more distinctive as Lawrence pulled his comforter over his head. Moreover, not just the smell of grass was profound at this point, but the deafening sound of a lawn mower engine increasingly annoyed Lawrence. He jumped out of his bed to close his bedroom window, and to close his blinds. Lawrence looked at his digital alarm clock, and the time read eight thirty-two. He then climbed back into bed. After enjoying the pleasant breeze from his window all night, it wasn't long before the temperature in his bedroom became uncomfortably warm. Lawrence sat on the side of his bed, frustrated that he had been awakened by his neighbor's lawn mower this early on a Saturday morning, when he usually slept much later. He lifted his bedroom window and yelled out to his neighbor, Enrique Cortez.

"Do you have to cut that damn lawn every Saturday morning so early while I am sleeping? Some of us have real careers, and do more than cutting lawns all day. I am a branch manager for Safeway National Bank. I work hard managing subordinates like you all week. I am entitled to have some peace on my weekends."

“So sorry, my friend, I cut your grass for free for your inconvenience,” Enrique said to make amends.

“Don’t touch my lawn. I have well-qualified landscapers for that already. If you want to do me a favor, wait at least until noon to cut your lawn on Saturdays,” Lawrence shouted.

“No problem, my friend. I cut later next time.”

Lawrence didn’t like Enrique or his family very much. He never spoke to any of them, even out of courtesy. However, when he’d come home from his job, where he was now seeking a corporate-level position, he would ask members of the Cortez family whether or not they’d seen any Amazon packages delivered to his home. Enrique and his family had moved in next door a little more than a year ago, and Lawrence, who often determined his association with others based on their prominence, was very disappointed with his new neighbors.

He decided he would start this day knowing it would take him quite a while to unwind enough to fall back to sleep. Lawrence usually took melatonin at night to aid him in getting a sufficient amount of sleep. He found it routinely difficult to shut his brain down from thinking while in bed. Therefore, he decided to prepare himself for the family gathering at his parents’ home later this afternoon. Lawrence didn’t particularly enjoy attending family gatherings, but his mother, Samantha, had penciled this event in on her calendar centered around Lawrence’s work schedule, because she really wanted him to attend and engage with family. If Lawrence had his way, he would continue to interact only with family members who had similar professional backgrounds. Whenever Lawrence would have dinner parties at his house, many family members who didn’t fit his profile were often excluded.

The parties he sponsored at his house were geared toward professional networking, and his perception of many in his family assured he would be embarrassed by their presence. Lawrence's cell phone rang, and he seemed aggravated by his own ring tone of Frank Sinatra singing *I Did It My Way* at this moment. He looked at his cell phone screen and saw it was his mother calling him.

"Hello, Mom, how are you this early Saturday morning?" Lawrence said, indicating to his mother that she had called him prematurely..

"Good morning, son, I took a chance hoping you were awake, because I need you to take care of something important for me. Were you sleeping, Lawrence.?"

"No, Mom, I cannot be asleep if I'm talking to you," Lawrence answered.

"You watch that sarcasm. You may be a big deal where you work, but I'm still your mother, not to be confused with employees that work for you. Anyway, I need you to go to the store for me because Denise was going to cook a pan of potato salad as a side dish, but she's not feeling well, so I have to do it for her."

Lawrence was quiet for a moment, but finally said, "Okay, Mom."

"I also need you to pick up your aunt Bethany and her two boys to drive them to our house for the family gathering. I was going to pick them up, but now that I'll be making the potato salad on top of cooking the smothered pork chops and green beans, I just can't do it all and be ready when my guests arrive."

"Mom, why are you cooking so much food for all these trifling people in the family? They will show up, eat everything in sight, take plates, and won't lift a finger to assist with anything," Lawrence asked.

"I'm doing it for the same reason your father and I paid for your college tuition. Now, you're going to pick up your aunt Bethany and her two boys because we're family."

Not totally satisfied with his mother's rationale, Lawrence shot back, "I don't know why you keep saying aunt Bethany and her two boys like her sons are toddlers or teenagers. They're two grown men that still live with their mother. Neither one of these men has ever owned a car. I don't mind picking up aunt Bethany, but Albert and Michael should feel ashamed that another man has to come to their house to pick up their mother and chauffeur her around."

Without totally considering Lawrence's point, Samantha responded, "Just do as I've asked you, son, and I guess I'll see you about noon with my grocery list. The guests are scheduled to arrive at two o'clock."

"Can I just pay for an Uber ride to pick them up?" Lawrence asked, trying to manipulate his way out of engaging with his cousins. "That way I can bring your groceries early and just catch up with Dad while he cooks his ribs on the grill in the yard."

"No, we're family, and we don't send strangers to do things we should be doing for one another. Now work on your interpersonal skills, and do as I've asked you." Samantha had a way of humbling her son in a way no one else could.

"Yes, ma'am, I'll see you at noon."

Lawrence showered, dressed, and left his house on the way to get a manicure and pedicure at Myteen Lee's Nail Shop, which he frequented every other Saturday morning. Lawrence had forgotten to make an appointment earlier in the week, and when he arrived, Min-jun, the nail technician who traditionally serviced his nails, was busy with another client.

Lawrence walked over to ask, "How many customers do you have ahead of me?"

Min-jun looked around and answered, "One here, two on way. You need make appointment. My cousin Jun-Young does good for you," Min-jun offered.

"No, I'll run to the store and come back in an hour-and-a-half. Will you be free at that time?" Lawrence asked.

Min-jun began to speak to other nail technicians in her native language. This always made Lawrence uncomfortable, especially when they would laugh, but he never said anything.

"Jun-Young do for you now if you like. If no like, I do for you when you come back." Unsatisfied with Min-jun's initial offer, Lawrence left the shop and pursued the grocery store, which was on the same block as the nail shop. He picked up all the items his mother had requested to make the potato salad, and he drove to his parents' home, which was thirty minutes away from his house.

He entered his parents' backyard through a side gate after seeing smoke, smelling barbecue, and hearing classic rhythm and blues music. Lawrence knew his father would be in the yard, and after he turned the corner of the house and stepped over the water hose, he walked over to greet his father. "Hey, Dad, I see you're getting it started while you're listening to your dusties."

Lawrence's father, Stanley, closed the vents on his barbecue grill and said, "Boy, set those bags down and give your old man a hug. I haven't seen you since New Year's."

Lawrence did as his father asked, embracing him, but his father held on to him for an extended time, way past the time Lawrence released his clinch.

"I've been busy, Dad. If I can get one of my subordinates to step up, I can really be up for a promotion. The branch I'm managing right now has to be covered properly before I can make my move. I have the opportunity to become a regional manager, and open up other branches in this state and throughout the United States."

Stanley's facial expression changed. "Subordinates, when the hell did you start referring to people as subordinates? And why are you dressed like you're going to a board meeting? This is a family barbecue."

Stunned by his father's comments but opting not to address the first question, Lawrence answered, "Dress like what, Dad? I called myself dressing down today. Believe me, Dad, these are not clothes I would wear to a meeting."

"Well, if that's dressing down, I hope you don't mind getting barbecue smeared on your expensive name-brand clothing. It's fine by me. I didn't buy them." Lawrence looked at his father with a perplexed look. "You told your mother you were coming by to shoot the breeze with me and help me barbecue before you go pick up your aunt Bethany and your cousins, right?" Stanley stood waiting on an answer from his son.

"Yes, I kind of said that, but I have to get back across town for my manicure." Lawrence didn't bother to say he was also getting a pedicure; he knew his father was already biased against men who obtained manicures at the same nail shop women often patronized.

"When your mom said you were going to help me out, I planned to go to the outlet to buy two gazebos that are on clearance. The sun is shining too brightly on the patio. I don't want our guests to be uncomfortable."

"Dad, I'm sorry, can't Reginald or Tony help you out? I've already made my appointment." It was obvious Stanley was disappointed with his son, whom he hadn't seen in several months, and it was evident by his facial expression. "Your brother Reginald doesn't get off work until six o'clock, and unfortunately Tony's car is in the repair shop. He's riding with his wife here later after their son's baseball game is over," Stanley explained.

"Why don't I go pick up the gazebos. I'll even pay for them, Dad, since I'm the cause of the mix-up."

"Not everything can be fixed with spending money, son. There are things that are a lot more important. Like time, relationships, and family." Stanley was a proud man, and he had lived very much by a select set of principles his entire life.

Stanley and Samantha had raised their four children in the Englewood area of Chicago. Lawrence and his sister Brianna had attended a private school on the north side of the Hyde Park area, but Lawrence's two brothers, Reginald and Tony, wanted to get their education in the public schools sector. They both played high school basketball, and they sought out the tough level of competition Chicago was known for. Reginald was two years older than Tony, and Tony was two years older than Lawrence. Lawrence was only eleven months older than Brianna.

Reginald graduated and was recruited to play college basketball for Chicago State University, and although college basketball was the end of the road for his basketball career, the relationships he developed through playing college basketball opened doors for him. Chicago State paid for eighty percent of his college tuition. He currently worked for the Chicago Transit Authority as a garage supervisor after initially driving a bus throughout the city for seven years.

His younger brother Tony married his high school sweetheart, Kolinda, shortly after graduation, after she became pregnant during their senior year of high school. Tony never fulfilled his aspirations of playing professional basketball after having two more children following their first child. Tony had worked in several menial positions, but those jobs were always high-turnover and low in pay, with poor working conditions. His wife, on the other hand, had become a successful real estate agent, and she invested a lot of her financial resources into her husband, who now ran his own newspaper and magazine stand. The business essentially mirrored the same financial bracket he was in when he worked for other companies. However, the difference was that now Tony was his own boss. He worked fewer hours, and his freedom allowed him to be home for their children. He was able to attend their children's extracurricular activities, and he thrived in the role of homemaker as Kolinda continued to build her real estate clientele.

Their complementary situation worked well for the both of them, and had saved their household thousands of dollars in childcare over the years. Lawrence rarely saw either of his brothers except for special occasions at their parents' home. However, he did communicate and interact with his sister Brianna regularly. They meet for lunch at a Greek restaurant that had become their favorite place to eat, and Lawrence visited Brianna and her husband Terrence's home frequently for dinner parties. He also made it a point to spend valuable time with their two children, Clarissa and Terri. Be that as it may, Lawrence didn't spend an equal amount of time with the nieces and nephews fathered by his two brothers. Lawrence was the only one of his parents' children who didn't have children of his own, and although he was quite fond of children, his alternative lifestyle served as a barrier to the traditional way of conceiving a child.

Brianna and Lawrence had always been closer than their other two siblings primarily because they were close in age, but growing up, the two also had many things in common. Their very close relationship kept Brianna from feeling inadequate about being the only girl in the family, along with being the youngest.

Lawrence's estranged relationship with his two brothers started when he was about twelve years old. He was on summer vacation from school, and his two brothers were away at a Penny Hardaway basketball camp in Memphis. With his two brothers being away for a few weeks, Lawrence was more relaxed, finally having peace of mind in their home. Both his brothers regularly antagonized him for his fascination with tea sets, but most notably because he didn't engage in sports the way they did.

During the boys' absence, their parents abandoned their once-a-week date night, because they didn't trust Lawrence and Brianna to be left home alone. But on this particular evening, Reginald and Tony returned home after being picked up by their father from the school drop-off. Knowing the two older boys would be home, the parents planned a date for dinner, to be followed by attending a movie. This bit of information was known by everyone in the family except Lawrence. Stanley helped his sons with their bags and their basketball gear into the house, and he straightaway yelled out to his wife, "Drop what you're doing! We're leaving early. It's our time tonight."

Samantha smiled, hugged and kissed her two sons, and informed them there was spaghetti and baked chicken on the stove for dinner. As soon as Tony dropped his bags in his room, he immediately went to Lawrence's room to hassle him the way he routinely did. To his surprise, Lawrence wasn't in his room, so he went to Brianna's room to say hello.

Upon opening Brianna's door, he saw Lawrence sitting at the table in Brianna's room engaging in what she called accessorizing her dolls' wardrobes, along with organizing her treasured tea sets. Tony yelled out to his older brother Reginald to be witness to what he discovered in Brianna's room. Lawrence's back was to the doorway where Tony stood waiting for his brother. When Lawrence stood up, he had on Brianna's blouse, and his fingernails were painted blue.

Brianna immediately yelled for Tony and Reginald to get out of her room, exercising the rule that her brothers were not allowed in her room unless she invited them in.

"Oh, we'll get out of your precious room, but he's coming with us," Reginald said as he pulled Lawrence out of the room by the collar of Brianna's blouse.

"Stop it. Leave him alone! You're going to tear my blouse!" Brianna screamed. "Stay in your room. You know we're in charge now. If you come out of your room, you're going to get exactly what he gets," Tony threatened.

Brianna was concerned for Lawrence, but she followed the instructions of her older brother out of fear, not out of respect. Lawrence struggled against being led out of the kitchen's back door, but now Tony assisted Reginald, as they lifted Lawrence under his arms and escorted him out to the garage.

"I'll take it off, I'll take it off," Lawrence yelled while being shoved into a chair. He was held by Reginald and tied to the chair with rope by Tony.

"Wait, I'm going to get the camera. Dad needs to see this," Tony yelled, and ran out of the garage and into the house to obtain the camera. Lawrence pleaded with Reginald not to tell their father that he was dressed in his sister's blouse, and that his nails were painted with fingernail polish. "Please don't tell Dad. I'll do anything you tell me to do."

"Oh, now you'll do anything I say. You mean like do all of our chores?" Reginald asked. "Yes, I'll do your chores, but please don't tell Dad."

Reginald pondered Lawrence's offer and decided to sweeten the pot since Lawrence was in this vulnerable position. "So, will you be our slave?" Lawrence didn't answer.

By this time Tony was back with the camera. "I brought some of Brianna's barrettes too. We can put them in his hair before we take the pictures," Tony said while laughing.

"I'll be your slave. Please don't do this."

Reginald stood behind Lawrence smiling and nodding his head toward Tony. "Okay, we'll accept your offer, but the first time we tell you to do something and it doesn't get done, we're going to tell Dad. We'll hold on to this picture for evidence. Tony, take his picture." Tony didn't know exactly what Reginald was orchestrating, but because he trusted his older brother and heard Lawrence say he would be their slave, he took the pictures without questions.

For the next six years until Lawrence left home for college, he was used, misused, and harassed by his older brothers. Reginald left home when he was nineteen and lost interest in needling his younger brother. However, Tony enjoyed every minute of exploiting Lawrence, even until the present day. It was because of this that Lawrence continued to have a massive amount of disdain for Tony.

Lawrence now sat in the massage chair with his eyes closed, thinking about the third annual unisex party he had been invited to, but turned down because he was expected by his parents to attend their family gathering.

"You no speak much today. Something with you wrong?" Min-jun asked while shaking Lawrence on his shoulder.

"Not really. It appears all my life I've done what other people wanted me to do, and at thirty-two years of age, I'm still living a lie of who I really am."

Min-jun tapped Lawrence's left foot to soak in the bowl while she elevated his right foot to the footrest.

"Why does it matter if you boy or girl, family love you anyway," Min-jun counseled.

"My sister does, and maybe my mother could handle my lifestyle, but I seriously doubt my brothers or my dad would be able to."

"Old proverb says the dog that chases his tail loses the bone," Min-jun said while massaging the heated stones on Lawrence's legs and feet.

"Lady, you've been drinking too much of that green tea. I don't know what the hell you're talking about," Lawrence said.

Min-jun dropped Lawrence's foot, which was resting on her thigh while she massaged his legs. "You people like dog, search for not real when the bone sits beneath you."

Lawrence thought about the revelation of Min-jun's parable, but he didn't utter a word. Then he simply responded, "Thank you."

After Min-jun finished Lawrence's manicure, he thanked her, paid her and left her a generous tip of fifty dollars for the value of the advice she'd given him.

Lawrence didn't associate with his family members or much of anyone he felt did not have equal or higher distinction than he possessed. He no longer was sour about picking up his two cousins with his aunt Bethany. His plan now was to stay at the family event for a few hours, then depart early to attend the unisex party, which was now becoming an anticipated tradition.

"I've done my due diligence. What else do they want from me. I'm gorgeous. I make one hundred-twenty thousand a year, I did the grocery shopping, and I'm allowing these unsavory characters to enter my 2020 Genesis G90. It's time I start doing things for me, and it starts today," Lawrence said while looking in his rearview mirror before pulling out. He was a bit behind schedule because Min-jun had taken a little longer with his pedicure and manicure than she normally did. Nonetheless, Lawrence resolved to arrive at his aunt's house at his own leisure.

Not too long after Lawrence left the nail shop, he arrived at Princeton Avenue and drove slowly up the block until he was in front of his aunt's house. Lawrence's car drew attention from a group of young men standing on the corner. Lawrence sounded his car horn, and his cousin Albert raised himself up from under the hood of a 1991 Oldsmobile Delta 88.

"Hey, what's up cousin. Well, that's a luxury car if I ever seen one. You're drawing too much attention, and not just from my mother," Albert stated with purpose.

"I know you are not parked in the middle of the street blowing your car horn in front of my house for me. Park your car, come in this house and speak to me properly. You need to help carry these bags also," Aunt Bethany yelled out of the screen door at her nephew Lawrence.

"I knew that was coming. Go ahead and pull that spaceship over and come on in and indulge with the have nots for a little while," Albert said mockingly.

Lawrence pulled into the parking space across from his aunt's house, and when he exited the car, he was still annoyed by Albert's comments. "Are you going? You're out here fixing cars and greased up. I'm ready to go now," Lawrence declared.

"Don't worry about me, barrettes, I'm ready. I just need to wash my hands and put on a shirt." Bristling at Albert's name calling, Lawrence shot back, "Don't call me that. We're not kids anymore. Besides, I don't think you're in any position to call anybody names with those worn-out shoes you have on."

Albert didn't take Lawrence seriously, because he had received this same type of response from Lawrence when they were kids whenever he would call him barrettes. That picture with Lawrence tied to a chair with his sister's blouse, his nails painted, and with barrettes in his hair circulated throughout the family for years. Barrettes became Lawrence's family nickname, but not in the presence of adults in the family at that time. After Lawrence was humbled by his aunt Bethany, he helped his cousins Michael and Albert carry what seemed like an entire buffet of food to his car. Lawrence was annoyed that Albert was working on a car upon his arrival. He wanted to ask why his cousin wasn't able to drive the car he was working on, whomever the car may belong to, but he knew whatever response Albert would give wouldn't be acceptable to him. Lawrence continued driving to his parents' home, while answering all of his aunt Bethany's prying questions. When he pulled into the driveway of his parents' home, his sister Brianna yelled out to him, "Dad said don't park in the driveway, because he wants Reginald and his wife to have a space to park when they come from Kenard's baseball game."

Lawrence got out of his car, and after greeting his sister with a hug and kiss, he stated in a low voice, "After I unload this smorgasbord, then I'll move my car." Lawrence helped his two cousins take the food to the backyard, where many of his other family members were now present.

They greeted him and wanted to display loving affection, but Lawrence spoke to everyone in general and exited the yard quickly. "I'll be back; I have to move my car." As soon as Lawrence entered his car, he could see the stains from the juice of the green beans his aunt had placed on the floor of the passenger side of his car. He was livid, but he had too much honor and respect for his aunt Bethany to confront her about staining his light brown interior.

Lawrence entered the yard, and he was motioned to the table where many of his aunts, uncles, and cousins were sitting.

"I know you're mister big shot now, but the next time you're around your family whom you haven't seen in God knows how long, those damn bags you were carrying better wait," Lawrence's Uncle Cedric stated.

"You pay him no never mind, come over here and give your Aunt Lucille a hug." Lawrence walked over and hugged his aunt as instructed. "Why don't you come around more often? And why aren't you married and have children like your brothers? You're not trying to be one of those playboys, are you?" Lucille said jokingly.

"No, ma'am, I'm not. I just haven't found the right person, and I'm not sure I even want to have children."

When Lawrence said he wasn't sure about having children, he received quite a few stares from many of his family members. His mother even looked at him strangely, because this was the first she had heard of this.

Tony immediately chimed in to break the silence. "Why are all of you guys acting surprised that Lawrence doesn't want to have kids? You would have to enjoy the pleasure of making the kids with a woman, of course. I plan on having at least two more before I'm done."

Tony's wife smacked him on his arm and immediately shot back, "I don't know who you're going to get to have these two children. Your baby-making days are over. This body is on permanent hiatus from little humans feeding off my body," Kolinda said with all seriousness.

Lawrence sat quiet for a moment while everyone seemed to go back to their conversations and their enjoyment of the music. Lawrence had his fill with being reduced by his family, only to appease them at his own expense. "So, who are you supposed to be, my judge and jury now? It's my damn choice if I want to have children or not. Who I enjoy having sex with is no business of yours. You choose to have it with a woman, but I choose to check the box marked other," Lawrence said, finally freeing himself from lifelong concealment.

"Other, what's that's supposed to mean, Lawrence?" his father asked.

"It means I'm gay, Dad, and that is not news to most of this family. If you would've made some effort to be as close to me the way you were with my two brothers, you would've known that already."

Stanley shook his head, indicating he was confused about what was taking place.

"So, you're gay now? You've climbed that ladder of success so high that you've been seduced into a forbidden lifestyle?" Cedric asked.

"Uncle Cedric, the only thing that's forbidden about the lifestyle that I live is the fact that my family forbid me from being what I am. As for the ladder of success, being a bank manager is not at all what I consider to be a ladder of success. I am seeking much higher goals than that, and if I was altered by success, I certainly wouldn't be here at this underprivileged form of entertainment."

Samantha was astonished that this was happening right now in front of family. Deep down she suspected her son was gay, but she always wanted him to feel comfortable enough to confide in her on his own, but certainly not in this way.

"Well, I'm glad Mr. High and Mighty finally came out the closet, but I hope you know that being gay is not your only issue," Tony said.

"You know what, Tony, you're right. I have just as many issues as you have. You're a paperboy, and you're thirty-four years old living off your wife."

The smirk that was on Tony's faced disappeared and was replaced with a look of agitation. "I don't live off my wife. I have my own business, whether you're aware of it or not. You work for someone, Mr. Big Shot. I'm my own boss."

Lawrence laughed cynically, knowing he'd pushed a button with Tony. "Your whole existence is dependent upon someone writing articles for the newspapers and magazines you sell. There is no creativity or pertinent performance in that. If they don't write or deliver to you, your entire business folds, and no one would ever know you existed."

Samantha finally intervened. "You two stop this foolishness right now. You're brothers, and whatever problems you have with one another, you love each other past it," Samantha said as she walked in between her sons and faced them both.

"I love my brother, Mom, even though he's always been a jerk to me. He just never amounted to anything more than a paperboy, and we need to stop acting like we don't know it. Moreover, ever since we were kids, he's always put me down and felt he was in a position to pass judgment on me." Tony was about to respond, but Samantha spoke before he could form his words.

"Brothers have disagreements, and brothers are often in competition with one another. But that still doesn't escape the fact that you are family, and in this family we are obligated to love and support each other," Samantha said with sincerity, her eyes watering with tears.

"He's my brother, but he's always been too sensitive. I already have one sister. I don't know why I always had to cater to his feelings because of what he is," Tony said angrily.

"I really don't know why I attend these gatherings anyway. Well, actually I do. Mom, Dad, I can no longer be where you want me to be anymore, because I feel I'm being tolerated and not celebrated. I have to be who I am, and my idea of fun is not being outside, constantly being bitten by mosquitos while pretending to be sociable with people who are not on my level," Lawrence explained cynically.

"So, we're not good enough for you anymore just because you live in a condominium, drive a fancy car and live in the so called affluent community?" Bethany asked.

"I love you aunt Bethany, but that just about sums it all up. It's all about the image, baby," Lawrence said, stepping back with his arms spread, inviting everyone to look at him. "As for that little fancy car you referred to, it wasn't at all little when I picked you and your grown children up this afternoon. By the way, it's no longer fancy now that you've leaked green bean juice all over my custom-made interior."

Albert walked around one of the patio benches and stood directly in front of Lawrence. "You might want to be mindful of how you speak to my mother. I don't want to have to disrespect your parents and their home the way you've disrespected my mother."

Lawrence took one step back and stated, "If you touch me, I'll have you arrested and I'll sue your ass."

Stanley had enough of this embarrassing sideshow. He now stepped in the middle between his nephew and Lawrence, nudging his son toward the house.

"Sorry, Dad, I can no longer endure these people, and I know you're disappointed in me. So, I am going to leave. There is a party I've been invited to by a multitude of people I can relate to," Lawrence said mockingly and headed toward the driveway. Before he completely exited the yard, he turned to his sister Brianna, winked, and affirmed, "I'll call you."

Lawrence left his parents' home feeling very much accomplished that for the first time in his life he had a sense of freedom about who he was and what his lifestyle entailed. He went to the unisex party as planned, pleased that he'd finally stood up to his brother, while revealing to his entire family his alternative lifestyle. That night at the party, Lawrence met a transgender person by the name of Royalty, and they danced, talked, and drank tequilas until two o'clock in the morning before Lawrence decided to leave.

Lawrence stopped drinking tequilas a little after midnight to give the drinks he'd consumed time to moderate before driving Royalty to her home. Shortly thereafter, due to the time of morning it was and there not being any traffic, Lawrence pulled into his driveway. His neighbor Enrique and most of the Cortez family were in the front yard cooking and playing music. The music was not disturbingly loud, and even the children who were still awake at this hour were conscious of their tone of voice while they played a mock game of soccer in their limited space..

Lawrence's mood immediately changed from contentment to being filled with rage. He slammed his car door and walked across Enrique's lawn past the children in the yard. He stood directly in front of the front porch, where many adults were dancing and talking.

"What the hell do you think this is? You're not in Mexico any longer, and you're playing that awful carnival music, which is piercing my soul. You already woke me up this morning running that lawn mower. Now you and your family are out here in what used to be a quiet community at nearly three in the morning having a Mexican parade. Either you tell your people to go inside or I'll be forced to call the authorities."

Enrique didn't take offense at Lawrence's statements, but many of his family members who understood English took exception. "Take it easy, hombre, let Maria make you a fresh guacamole burger and have a tequila on me, my friend," Enrique offered.

"If I call the police, someone is probably going to get deported. I know everyone attending this fiesta is not legal in this country," Lawrence said firmly, with total insensitivity.

"Why you have to be mean, bro? I try to be nice to you, but you insult me and my family. Get off my property before I let the homeboys make new artwork out of you. Call the cops if you want." The smile Enrique normally displayed was nowhere in sight as he walked toward where Lawrence was standing.

Lawrence could see he had struck a chord with Enrique and his family members, many of them now standing and staring at Lawrence with contempt. Lawrence quickly walked across Enrique's lawn in the direction of his house. He was reluctant to call the police, because he could tell he had insulted the Cortez family, and he was not ready to deal with the backlash that contacting the police was sure to add. Although Lawrence earlier had been engaged in verbal altercations with his own family members, it had now transferred over to his neighbors.

Regardless, he felt he was totally within his rights to be free to be openly gay, and after his breathtaking experience at the unisex party, he was determined to live his life with no restraints going forward. He enjoyed the remainder of his weekend, and Sunday he mentally prepared himself for his upcoming work week.

Monday morning Lawrence was in his office at the bank when one of his bank tellers entered his office without knocking. "My office door was minimally ajar for a reason. I highly suggest you knock on my office door before entering the next time," Lawrence said in a testy voice.

"I apologize, but we have a difficult customer out here, and he is really being rude and causing a scene. I witnessed Jill follow every bank protocol with the customer, but he continues to escalate and requested to speak to the manager,"

Rachel, the assistant manager, explained.

Lawrence didn't ask any other questions. He rose from his seat and simply stated while walking toward the front of the bank at a fast pace, "What good is it for me to have an assistant manager if I have to handle and address everything myself?"

"I did address it, sir, but he wanted to speak to the manager in charge of the bank," Rachel responded.

When Lawrence walked onto the floor, he could hear the customer yelling as he stood at the counter in front of Jill. "No, I'm not moving. I haven't been served properly, and I still have yet to speak to someone in charge," the man said, obviously seeking to draw attention.

"Excuse me, sir, my name is Lawrence, and I'm the bank manager for Safeway. What seems to be the problem?" Lawrence said while looking at the customer's mangled attire.

"Your cashier has a problem giving me my money the way I asked for it. Why would you cash a check and give someone two one hundred dollar bills? I asked for smaller bills, and fifty single dollar bills, but what she gave me was attitude," the customer said loudly. Now there were only two other customers in the bank.

"What is your name, sir?" Lawrence asked.

"My name is Antonio," the customer responded.

"Thank you, Antonio, and what is your last name, sir?"

Antonio looked at Lawrence with a penetrating look as he positioned himself directly in front of Lawrence at this point. "My last name is Cortez, and I told you already my name is Antonio. Why are you calling me 'sir'? I hope I didn't make a mistake by asking to speak to the manager."

Lawrence forced a smile, then stated, "I assure you, Mr. Cortez, you did not make a mistake. You're talking to the man who will resolve any issues you may have. Can you step over into this cubicle so we can talk further in private?"

"You mean you manage this entire bank, and you're still stuck in a cubicle like this subservient woman?" Antonio said while looking at the cashier Jill in front of him.

Keeping his poise, Lawrence explained calmly, "They're bank tellers, sir, and yes, I do have an office, but I thought it would be more convenient to step right over here instead of walking to the back where my office is."

"Well speak for yourself, cowboy. I'd rather sit in one of those executive chairs and drink some of that expensive coffee you have in your office. Not this brown piss you guys set out here for customers."

"Speaking of customers, do you have an account here?" Lawrence seized the opportunity to ask Antonio.

"No, I don't have an account here. But the check I cashed is from this bank, and if you help me out, I can open up an account with you guys today. That sign outside says you'll give me one hundred dollars if I open an account."

Lawrence's level of irritation was starting to show once Antonio said he didn't have an account with Safeway National Bank. He no longer felt the need to be as cordial and professional to Antonio. "Sir, you don't have to talk so loud, and that one hundred dollars to open a checking account comes with conditions. The account must be maintained for at least six months, and you must maintain a minimum balance of one hundred dollars." Antonio took two lollipops out of the container sitting on the desk as he sat down.

"Oh, so you guys up in here scamming people, huh? Sounds like nothing short of being an Indian giver to me. You give someone something, then control what the person does with the money you gave them."

"First of all, that statement is offensive to the Native Americans of this nation, but more importantly, what can I help you with today, sir?" Lawrence said, staying on task.

"I asked you not to call me sir. Is everyone in this damn bank deaf and dumb?" Antonio said, and snickered afterwards.

Lawrence took a deep breath, then said once again, "So what can I help you with today, sir?"

"I was thinking about opening one of those Roth INA's for my retirement," Antonio answered.

"I think you mean Roth IRA, and what kind of work do you do sir?"

"Well, I'm kind of between jobs right now, but I do pretty good on my food cart every week. I park right outside of UPS, and their employees eat their breakfast and lunches with me. They all say my food tastes better than their cafeteria food and it's cheaper as well. I could sell you some churros and corn if you'd like," Antonio continued.

"So basically, all you want is fifty singles, because you're wasting my time. I have a bank to run, and I am not about to contribute to you soliciting food in my bank, and I'm willing to bet you have no permit as a food vendor," Lawrence said in a condescending manner.

"You're not supposed to speak to me that way, my friend. You're supposed to be like, how you say, professional," Antonio said, feeling offended.

"Sir, do you want me to cash out your fifty dollars for singles or not? I've gone just about as far as I can go with you," Lawrence said with all seriousness.

"No, I've gone about as far as I will go with you. I am Antonio Cortez and I am the VP Corporate Treasurer for Safeway Bank. I understand you were looking to make the next move beyond branch manager. As luck would have it, my colleagues and I were viewing your impressive profile in banking. We just started going to different branches across the state to see how many of our banks operate on a daily basis. From tycoon billionaire bank accounts to the minimal checking accounts we offer our customers. I must say, Lawrence, your bank tellers were exceptional the way they handled such a difficult client, and they followed every one of Safeway's protocols. Unfortunately, your staff are not a representation of the branch manager. You failed miserably in your treatment of a potential customer when you found out I didn't have an account, and that I was self-employed.

"You must know that Safeway National Bank has excelled for more than a hundred years, not only because of large corporations, but because of small businesses and self-employed individuals. We don't subscribe to you telling any customer that they're wasting your time. I'll be submitting my findings in a detailed report, and you'll be hearing from corporate some time real soon," Antonio Cortez explained.

"Mr. Cortez, I am embarrassed by my behavior. I have no excuses but I had an awful weekend, although my weekend shouldn't filter over into our banking business. I greatly apologize for my rude disposition. This is not how I normally operate. Ask any of my employees," Lawrence said with submissiveness.

"I would certainly hope not," Antonio followed.

"I hope this doesn't affect my chances of moving up, sir, as you said my profile is accomplished and I'm only thirty-two years old."

Antonio smiled and stated, "Oh, it will no doubt put a blemish on your aspirations. I'm baffled as to how you've gotten this far with that kind of attitude. What you may deem as small contributions to our society can be enormous contributions to our society. Even if it's as miniscule as a landscaping business that entails cutting grass every day, especially on Saturday mornings."

It was at that moment Lawrence was able to put together that Antonio's last name was associated with his neighbor Enrique, and Antonio Cortez's comment about landscaping was a direct result of Lawrence's altercation with the Cortez family over the weekend.

The Issue of Being **Institutionalized**

Chapter 4

GWENDOLYN DODD SAT IN the windowsill of her room watching employees and patients walk across the parking lot to the emergency room at Barrington Hospital. She'd just finished reading a letter that her father, whom was absent her entire life, had written to her. Gwendolyn was two years of age when her father was arrested, charged, and sentenced to twenty years of incarceration due to driving under the influence of alcohol, which led him to killing another man who was traveling home from work. Gwendolyn's mother passed away three years after her father was incarcerated, and she was raised by foster parents until she was thirteen years of age.

Gwendolyn began exhibiting defiant behavior toward her foster parents as she became older. She had feelings of hurt and anger for not having the opportunity to be with her family as many of her friends were. Unexplainably she became bitter toward Robert and Vanessa Stevenson, her foster parents, instead of having gratitude that the Stevensons had assumed full custody of her and raised her as their very own child. Her reckless behavior wasn't limited toward just her foster parents, but she exhibited increasingly defiant behavior at school as well.

After having many of her privileges taken away due to poor grades and being issued a five-day suspension from school, to make matters worse, Gwendolyn angrily set fire to her parents' home. Gwendolyn purposely poured rubbing alcohol on the carpet from her parents' bedroom to the bathroom. She then lit the carpet with her father's cigarette lighter that she'd taken off the dining room table. The Stevenson family lost their home to the fire, and the entire family was forced to move in with Vanessa's parents.

The family was at Vanessa's parents' home for nearly a week when Gwendolyn placed their cat in the dryer for five minutes after the cat scratched her. It was at this point Robert and Vanessa decided they could no longer endure her maladaptive behaviors, and they relinquished their role as guardians and foster parents. It became painfully clear to the Stevenson family that they were being blamed for Gwendolyn's hurt and anger toward and about her parents. They knew the misdirected anger would only persist..

In the letter from her father, which was given to her by a social worker from the hospital, Gwendolyn learned that he was being released on parole in sixty days. She had spoken to her father once on the telephone when she lived with her foster parents, but the past three years she had only communicated with him twice, and those times were handwritten letters just like the current letter.

There was a knock at the door to Gwendolyn's room, followed by a petition from one of the hospital staff members. "Gwendolyn, we're about to have dinner. We'd really like it if you would join us in the dining area," Ilya, one of the mental health counselors who worked in the adolescent psychiatry department for the hospital, said.

Gwendolyn still did not answer after a second knock and appeal, so Ilya opened the room door to ensure patient safety.

"I didn't give you permission to open my bedroom door. Get the fuck out of here."

The facial expression on Ilya's face changed before she took a step inside of Gwendolyn's room. "I knocked on your door out of courtesy. I do not need your permission to enter. It's imperative that we know that you're safe at all times. As far as this being your room, this is not your group home or your placement. You're simply occupying this space until you've received the treatment you were admitted for. Upon discharge back to your place of residence, you may claim ownership of the room assigned, but this room belongs to Barrington Hospital. Now, are you going to come to dinner in the dining room and join the community for dinner?"

Gwendolyn pondered Ilya's stance for a moment, then stated, "I'm not hungry. I'll eat later." She quickly changed her mind and asked, "I'll come out to eat, but what are we having for dinner?"

Ilya answered her quickly. "I wasn't present when you filled out your menu, young lady. It's been less than twenty-four hours. You should remember what you selected to eat for the day."

Gwendolyn hopped down from the windowsill she was sitting on that was also connected to the radiator in her room. "Not so fast, young lady. What are we going to do about your use of profanity? You know the use of profanity goes against the rules of this program," Ilya explained.

"Why are you always so thirsty to give someone a consequence? Why can't you just let it go? It's not like you never used curse words when you were my age," Gwendolyn shot back.

"See, that's the wrong answer and attitude. If you would've apologized and taken responsibility for your behavior, I would have been willing to, as you say, let it go. But since your answer to everything is blame and attack, we can discuss a loss of privileges after dinner. This is exactly why you have been here for two months when the normal length of stay is fourteen to twenty-one days."

Gwendolyn walked past Ilya down the corridor of the unit in exaggerated fashion, and as she walked past the nursing station, she knocked the phone off the desk and proceeded to pull at the telephone cord until it was dislodged from the wall. Gwendolyn walked into the dining area and sat next to another patient whom she had known from a stretch they had together while living in a group home in Westchester, Illinois, prior to Gwendolyn's step up to a more restrictive placement. There were two male staff members already in the dining area with all of the other patients who were trying to figure out where the loud disturbance was coming from.

"She needs to be escorted to the seclusion room. Karen has already called for support from the other units, and she's calling her doctor now to get an order for her to receive a PRN to help calm her down," Ilya explained.

"Gwendolyn, are you going to be able to walk to the seclusion room on your own, and avoid anyone having to physically escort you?" Carl asked.

"I'll walk on my own, but I'm going to eat my food first."

David, whom Gwendolyn had a good rapport with more so than any other members of the treatment team, walked over to where she was sitting and said, "I understand you received a letter from your father today. I know you must be having some feelings about the letter, and rightfully so. But you have to learn how to handle conflict and your emotions by communicating your feelings without escalating to aggression." Gwendolyn didn't respond as she continued to stuff large portions of food into her mouth.

"All right, ladies and gentlemen, we're having a bit of a crisis right now. I need for each of you to transition to your room, and when the crisis is over, we'll call everyone back out to finish having dinner," Ilya said.

"She does this shit every time, and we have to go to our room while you guys deal with her. You guys give her all the attention she wants, and she still acts like a spoiled-ass brat," a female patient by the name of Adriana declared as she stared at Gwendolyn.

Ilya guided Adriana by the arm and escorted her down the hall to her room while the other patients were able to transition on their own accord.

"Come on, Gwendolyn, make a good decision here. You're in control of this entire situation. It's your decision how all this will play out," David encouraged. Immediately after David finished his statement, multiple staff members from other units entered the room from both the rear and front exit doors.

Gwendolyn took two big gulps of the macaroni salad that was on her dinner tray, and then she rose up, walked out of the dining area, down the hall, and into the observation room.

"Your doctor has ordered you twenty-five milligrams of Thorazine to help calm you down. Your nurse will be in shortly to administer the medication. Are you going to be compliant, or are you going to fight like last time?" Carl asked. Gwendolyn faced Carl but didn't answer.

When Maxine, the charge nurse, entered the observation room, Gwendolyn immediately sat down on the leather bed usually purposed for restraints. "So, Ms. Gwendolyn, how are we going to do this? Are you going to take the medication willingly, or do these fine gentlemen have to assist me in administering the PRN?"

"Why do I have to take a shot? I'm calm now. Can't I just take a pill?" Gwendolyn asked.

"Well, this is what your doctor ordered, and if you have the ability to calm yourself on command, then the aggressive outburst you exhibited wouldn't have happened. So, I'm asking you, can you be compliant and take the medication without fighting?" Maxine asked once more, but Gwendolyn sighed and began swinging her feet, an indication her anxiety level was increasing. That had been a telltale sign for Gwendolyn prior to attacking staff members. Ilya walked out of the observation room without saying a word.

"So, what's it going to be, Gwendolyn?" Maxine asked, taking a step back, assuming Gwendolyn was about to attack the way she had Stephen, a coworker who was currently on Workman's Compensation leave after being attacked by Gwendolyn.

"So, what are we doing here? Is she going to take the medication or not? I have to get back to my unit," Greg said, becoming impatient with this approach.

David shook his head, disapproving of Greg's blunt statement that could further escalate the situation, but before Gwendolyn or anyone else could add anything else to the situation, Ilya re-entered the observation room with the blue bag that contained a set of Velcro restraints. Although the restraints weren't visible just yet, all the staff members and Gwendolyn were very much aware of what the blue transport consisted of.

Taking an unorthodox approach that went against crisis protocol, David walked over to Gwendolyn and whispered to her, "Please make a good decision right now. I don't want to see these guys put their hands on you or see you having to be placed in restraints for aggression." Gwendolyn hopped up and flipped her body over on the leather bed face down. Her movement was so sudden that David and Maxine flinched in response. "I'm taking the shot. No one better fucking touch me," Gwendolyn said in a clipped voice.

Maxine walked over apprehensively. "I'm going to pull your sweat pants to the side if that's all right. Let me prep you first with this alcohol pad, and just relax," Maxine instructed as she entered the needle into the ventrogluteal buttock muscle. After Maxine had successfully given the injection to Gwendolyn, she left the observation room to discard the syringe safely and was followed by other staff members exiting the room.

Gwendolyn yelled out, "Mr. David, can you stay and talk to me for a few minutes? I was compliant the way you asked, and I am calm."

Feeling safe, David answered immediately, "Yes, I can talk to you."

"Why don't you let her take her timeout, let her calm down, and allow the medication to begin to work before you talk to her?" Ilya suggested.

"It's fine. I can talk to her if she can contract for safety," David added, looking at Gwendolyn.

"I promise I'm calm. I'm not going to do anything, Mr. David. If I was going to do anything, it would be toward a staff member I don't like," Gwendolyn said, making an indirect threat toward Ilya. Gwendolyn knew full well a direct threat of harm could lead to her being restrained for two hours, so she didn't even look in Ilya's direction. Ilya was peeved that David did not adhere to her suggestion, and once again David was breaking program protocol by staying in the observation room alone with a patient before she had the opportunity to calm down.

While in the observation room, Gwendolyn convinced David that writing her father a reply letter would serve as a coping skill for her. David exited the observation room to obtain paper and pencil for the letter. The hospital policy stated that patients of the adolescent psychiatry department were prohibited use of pens and pencils. Patients were to use markers and crayons as an alternative to write. David stuck his hand into the plastic multi-tool box where the markers and crayons were stored, but he already had a pencil in his pocket to give to Gwendolyn. This was obviously part of David's deception, as he often deviated from the guidelines by which the treatment team operated. David felt the need to be accepted by the adolescent patient population, and this was the only way he knew how to do that.

David re-entered the observation room and handed Gwendolyn the marker and some paper with his back toward the camera. "I thought you said you were going to let me use a pencil. I can't use a marker to write an entire letter. David dropped the pencil on the leather bed and turned all in one motion to exit the observation room.

"I'll just remain here and monitor her outside the door until she's completely calm," David declared, while rolling one of the office chairs by the observation room door.

"There's no need for you to do that. We can see everything she does on the monitor," Ilya chimed in, knowing David had some ulterior motive, but she wasn't altogether sure what it was. David heard what Ilya said, but he sat down in the chair and periodically looked inside the small view window to check in on Gwendolyn.

More than a week went by, and Percy Dodd, Gwendolyn's father, sat on his bunk waiting for the call to be released for the inmate count, and to be escorted to the cafeteria for breakfast. After fifteen years of being incarcerated, the last two years Percy had the privacy of having his own space with no cellmate. Percy was very organized and tidy, with a limited amount of possessions that he was allowed to have. He had three pictures on the stick board against his cell wall. He had a picture of his mother, Margaret, who was advancing in age, a picture of his brother, Elgin, who had been his lone support system the entire fifteen years he'd been incarcerated, and a picture of his daughter, Gwendolyn, when she was just two months old. Percy's three state property uniforms and his overall suit for his job in distribution were all folded neatly in one pile, with five pair of white sweat socks on top of them.

He made sure his bunk and the bunk below him displayed creased folding of his sheets and blankets in the style of a military soldier. Percy was becoming restless, but then one of the correctional officers' voices rang out.

"Open block C," Officer Ramirez yelled. The clamp was released, followed by the doors opening. Percy stepped out of his cell and stood on the designated count line waiting for further instructions from Officer Ramirez. Percy routinely didn't eat the entrée portion of his breakfast meal. He would eat the box of cereal and drink his milk, but habitually he traded his entrée for something of more value to him, like cigarettes or toiletries. There was an obese man in cell block D named Elbert who used to be an accountant. He had been incarcerated for embezzling money from the company he worked for. He would typically bypass other inmates to get to a table in the hunt for Percy's breakfast. Elbert would purchase a list of commissary items for Percy in exchange for a week of his breakfast entrées.

Percy would pour the contents of his box of Raisin Bran into his milk carton after taking a swallow of his milk, and then he would open both ends of the container. After he set his tray in front of Elbert, who was sitting four rows down, he exited the dining area without any form of communication between the two. It was already understood and agreed upon that Elbert would just order the items given to him on Sunday night. On Monday after dinner, Elbert would bring those items to Percy's cell if it was permitted by one of the evening guards.

When Percy left the dining area, he passed by Officer Johnson and spoke to him in his customary fashion. "Top of the morning to you, Officer Johnson. How are you on this fine day?"

Officer Johnson had a mutual amount of respect for Percy, because during the four years he'd worked for the correctional facility, he'd never had any trouble from Percy, who had always followed his instructions without hesitation. Officer Johnson didn't care much for the younger inmates, because he felt they lacked respect and discipline.

"Percy, you know we don't distribute mail until after breakfast on Mondays, but since I personally inspected your mail and you're crossing my path now, I'll allow you to have it this time. But don't get used to this, inmate. You're nothing special," Officer Johnson said, maintaining his authoritative position.

"I would never take advantage of your unwavering generosity, Officer Johnson. I greatly appreciate your kindness," Percy said, exhibiting the same manner of reverence that he displayed toward all of the correctional officers. Early on in Percy's time, when he was at the Cook County Correctional Facility, he was angry. He had something to prove to other inmates, and he often challenged the correctional officers there. He was then moved to a maximum-security prison in Crest Hill, Illinois, called Statesville Correctional Center. On his second day at Statesville, he stabbed another inmate in the neck with a pencil after being commanded to sit at another table after he sat down. Thinking he needed to establish himself, Percy stabbed the other inmate for all to see. Fortunately, the stab wound did not puncture the inmate's main artery, and the man Percy stabbed gave a statement that he was trying to kill himself because he was depressed. He declared that Percy was just trying to remove the pencil from his hand, and that's what their struggle was about.

The inmate's name was Marcus Colfax, and after he was released from medical, he was transferred to Elgin Mental Health Center to treat his diagnosed psychiatric needs. Marcus seized the incident as a strategic ploy to get out of the correctional system where he had been sentenced to serve five years.

Shortly thereafter, Percy was mentored by an older inmate by the name of Walter Mounds, who witnessed the entire incident and regularly cautioned Percy not to add more time to his sentence the way he himself had done. The two became really close, and Percy commonly referred to him as Uncle Walt.

Officer Johnson handed Percy his mail. He thanked Officer Johnson once again and scurried back to his block, where he entered his cell and dived onto the bottom bunk to read his letter. It wasn't often that he received mail, but he could clearly see this letter was from his daughter Gwendolyn. He began reading the letter, hoping for the communication he'd been trying to establish with his daughter. In past years, Gwendolyn had made contact to communicate with Percy through letter writing, but then she would abruptly discontinue her communication. Three years ago, Gwendolyn wrote her father and told him how angry she was that she had to live in foster care and group homes because he wasn't a responsible father.

What Percy did not know was that although these were Gwendolyn's feelings, she was instructed by her therapist to write him, to tell him of her hurt feelings to serve as a form of therapy for her. The therapist also wanted Gwendolyn to address and acknowledge the anger she felt about having a void for her parents. The initial plan was to lay a foundation of communication built on trust to eliminate superficial relationships. After reading two paragraphs of his daughter's letter, Percy's anxiety seemed to decrease. Gwendolyn informed him that she had been hospitalized to a psychiatric hospital with a behavior modification program for adolescents the past two months, after escaping from her current residential. While on the run from her placement with two other girls, the three stole a car that was left running by a man paying for gas at a gas station. He left the nozzle dispensing gas, then went inside to pay for the gas and to play the lottery. Gwendolyn and her peers immediately jumped in the car and sped off.

Inside the armrest of the man's Honda Accord they found one hundred and sixty dollars in a bank envelope. Following the lead of one of the girls she was with, named Jennifer, on where to purchase marijuana, Gwendolyn drove to the Austin Community, where Jennifer had lived for four years with a foster family. Jennifer knew the area well and briefly interacted with people she knew. They not only directed her to a different location where marijuana of a higher quality was being sold, but Jennifer's foster brother's friend Darnell offered to pay for the marijuana if they would drive him to the liquor store to purchase alcohol. He invited them to accompany him and his friends, who were having what he called a get-together at the circle. Darnell took a liking to Michelle, the other girl who had escaped with Gwendolyn and Jennifer. They sat in the back seat and became intimately acquainted on the short drive to the circle. The tale of events that ensued that evening led to Gwendolyn's current hospitalization and the letter she was writing her father.

Percy lay on his bed staring up at the top bunk. He released the letter from his hand, and it fell to the floor. In his previous letter to his daughter, whom he'd only been in contact with twice in the past three years since she had been removed from her foster parents, Percy informed Gwendolyn that he was being released in less than sixty days. In her follow-up response, Gwendolyn asked her father once he found a place to live, could she come live with him. Percy was floored by this unexpected plea, considering Gwendolyn's lack of communication with him the past three years due to her anger toward him. It wasn't that Percy didn't want his daughter to live with him. His apprehension rested on whether he could provide for her, and he knew the Department of Children and Family Services would not allow a convicted felon to have sole custody of his daughter. More importantly, how could he explain to Gwendolyn that after being absent from him for fifteen years, her aspiration to live with him would not be merited. Percy was already trying to figure out how he was going to get a job and an apartment, and lastly how to get his mother Margaret to come live with him without losing her government benefits while living in an assisted living program.

Today was Gwendolyn's staffing day at Barrington Hospital, and she planned to be just as non-compliant and difficult as she had been the past eight weeks. Gwendolyn purposely made threats to escape in a previous staffing upon return to her residential. She boasted about the high-risk behaviors she planned to engage in the moment she was discharged from the hospital. She made these threats to negate any plans of discharge back to her placement. Gwendolyn was escorted by the charge nurse and the hospital social worker to the staffing in the conference room down the south hall of the unit.

When she entered the conference room, she didn't speak to anyone. Her doctor, placement therapist, and the director from her residential were all present in the conference room upon her arrival.

Gwendolyn brandished an enormous smirk on her face as she set to mock the meeting by acting out the way she had in times before. "Hello, Gwendolyn," Erica Langston, the director at her placement, said.

"Hi," Gwendolyn responded, without making eye contact with Erica.

"Hi, Gwendolyn, how are you today?" Bettye Wells, who was Gwendolyn's DCFS caseworker, spoke through the conference phone positioned on the table.

Gwendolyn was shocked to hear Bettye's voice. Usually Bettye was present when Gwendolyn would enter the conference room for her weekly hospital staffing. "Hi, Ms. Wells. Why aren't you here for my staffing this week?"

Mary, the social worker, pulled the conference phone closer to Gwendolyn so that she could hear and be heard clearly for those patched through the conference call.

"I apologize for not being able to be present today. I had to drive to Decatur, Illinois, to visit a client who's been having some challenging issues. But I have some great news for you, and I believe you will like what I have to say. It will require you to do a bit of work, but I believe you'll see the value in it."

Everyone in the room displayed a superficial smile as a way of encouraging Gwendolyn to buy into what Ms. Wells was pitching. Gwendolyn had been in the hospital for eight weeks, and every time she would get close to being discharged, she would act out aggressively or make threats to harm herself.

"Hello, Gwendolyn, I'm on the line too," Ramsey Banks, Gwendolyn's *guardian ad litem*, spoke through the conference phone. "I think you're going to like what Bettye has to say. I've worked really hard with her to get the okay for this, and she's right. You have to do a little work for this to happen." Gwendolyn was really uninterested in anything Ramsey and Bettye were trying to pitch to her, but because she really liked Bettye and had respect for her among very few people, she was prepared to listen to the snow job she was all set to reject.

"So, what do you think, Gwendolyn. Do you think you're ready to get on the right track so you can get the things you want?" Dr. Welyki asked.

"Am I ready for what? They haven't said anything yet. You're supposed to be a doctor and you have no listening skills," Gwendolyn said.

"Gwendolyn, let's get off on the right foot. I believe you're really going to want to hear what I have to say. Please apologize to Dr. Welyki so we can move on," Bettye said.

Gwendolyn bristled at the idea of an apology, and asked, "Why do I have to apologize to her? She's always saying stupid stuff, and I don't understand half of what she's saying anyway. How are you going to be in the United States as a doctor and you can hardly speak the language?" Gwendolyn continued.

"See, Gwendolyn, it's that kind of anger that has led you to make the decisions that keep you coming back to this hospital. We talked about making healthier choices. Now can you please apologize to Dr. Welyki?"

Gwendolyn sat back in her chair with her arms folded, displaying a frown on her face. "It's okay, Bettye. She doesn't have to apologize to me. No matter how rude she is to me, I'll always do what's best for her."

Gwendolyn took a deep breath, and then she finally uttered, "I'm sorry." She never made eye contact with Dr. Welyki in her pressured, insincere apology.

"I accept your apology," Dr. Welyki said, continuing to smile.

"Thank you, Gwendolyn," Bettye said. "I know you can do these things. That was very mature of you to make the decision to apologize. Now, the treatment team at the hospital, Ramsey, and I have worked diligently to get this approved, and it took a bit of doing, but now the ball is in your court." Gwendolyn was beginning to become irritated by the buildup, since no one had exactly said what this news entailed or what she was being asked to do. In the past, there had been created plans for Gwendolyn like stepping back down to a group home from a residential if she wouldn't have any hospitalization from harm to others or herself in a six-month period.

Those plans weren't acceptable to Gwendolyn, who felt like the only thing that would make her conform to these kinds of incentive plans was if she could live with her father, who was incarcerated, or live with another family member. However, no family members on either her mother's or her father's side of the family were willing to take on that responsibility because of her maladaptive behaviors.

"As you know, your father will be released in a few short weeks," Bettye said. "I know you have a desire to live with him, but there are many precipitating factors as to why this cannot happen right now. Your father is a convicted felon, and you must be in the care of someone who does not have a criminal background. Not to mention your father has to get things in order in his own life to even be considered to have visitation with you. As I understand it, he will be living with his sister until he finds a job. Hopefully at that point he could save money to get his own place, and that takes time. After speaking with your dad's sister and your Aunt Bernadette, the family plans to throw your dad a welcome home party at a forest preserve upon his release. Your entire family will be there, including your grandmother, who currently lives in an assisted living facility. I have been granted permission to take you to this welcome home party for your dad, provided you achieve the goals of this new plan."

Gwendolyn perked up and was now sitting on the edge of her seat waiting to hear the expectations she must meet. "So, what do I have to do for this to happen?"

Dr. Welyki smiled, because she could see Gwendolyn was showing interest.

"Well, Gwendolyn, if you are able to remain safe without aggression or self-harm within the next two weeks, Dr. Welyki will discharge you back to New Direction Residential," Erica, the director at New Direction Residential, chimed in. Gwendolyn flopped back into her chair and grunted, displaying her disappointment. "Wait, just listen. Hear me all the way out, Gwendolyn." Gwendolyn looked up at Erica but didn't say anything. "Once you're discharged from the hospital and you come back to Safeway, continue to remain safe, and follow the rules with no incidents, after those two weeks we're going to try out an independent living program. You will share an apartment with another young lady, and you two will be checked on spontaneously without notification to make sure you're following the guidelines of the program. If that continues to go well, you'll be turning seventeen in less than a month. It'll take your dad at least a year to get on his feet. In one year from now you could have all that you've been asking for," Erica said.

"In a year I'll be eighteen, so I don't need to jump through all those hoops. I'll be able to see my father and family on my own, because I'll be an adult," Gwendolyn shot back with arrogance.

"Well, that's not exactly true, Gwendolyn. You haven't exactly proven you can be stable, and you are still a ward of the state. Your high-risk behaviors signify you're not ready to be on your own just yet, even at eighteen."

"Nonetheless, you'll have the option to emancipate yourself from the state, but that will be at the discretion of the courts. As your personal attorney, I'm telling you this is a more viable option for you," Ramsey stated, trying to educate his client.

Gwendolyn could see there was a carrot being dangled in front of her, but there had been enough said that she felt she had to chase it. Left with limited options to get what she wanted, Gwendolyn said, "I'll follow the plan, but you guys better not be jerking me around about this independent living thing, because if you are, someone will definitely answer for that, I promise." Gwendolyn then rose from her seat to walk out of the conference room. The social worker and nurse quickly moved to escort her back to the unit.

The next seven days in Gwendolyn's treatment stay went by without any incidents or behavioral issues from her. She was compliant with staff, the unit rules, and her medication. She displayed no forms of aggression and made no threats to Dr. Welyki or any other staff members. The night before Gwendolyn was scheduled for discharge to return to her placement in the morning, she was assisted by Ilya with packing her clothing and items obtained during her hospitalization. Ilya told Gwendolyn to remind the staff members that would be present when she left in the morning about the items that belonged to her, which were not permitted on the unit with such high risk patients.

"Make sure when you get up to shower and have your breakfast to let my coworkers know immediately to obtain your oil sheen and body sprays from the cabinet inside of the medication room. If you don't remind them to put these things with the rest of your belongings, they'll more than likely forget to add them," Ilya explained.

"I won't forget, and Ms. Ilya, I want to say I'm sorry for punching you, and I'm sorry for giving you a hard time while I was here."

Ilya was extremely surprised Gwendolyn was apologizing for her behavior. Gwendolyn had been hospitalized several times in the past three years for her aggressive behavior, but she had never departed with an effort of peacemaking.

"Well, I'm not going to say I accept your apology. What I will say is the Gwendolyn you've displayed this past week is a person I have grown to like, and actually abstracted enjoyment out of working with. You were very positive in my groups, and you began to take responsibility for the things you can control. I've never seen you do that before, which leads me to the next thing I am about to say to you. Gwendolyn, you had the ability to conduct yourself appropriately all along. Now that they've given you a plan you feel is acceptable to you, you've found healthy and alternative ways of dealing with your anger. Again, I say, you had the ability to do this all along. If you have a setback, and for some reason need to come back to us for help, I look forward to working with and investing in this side of Gwendolyn, whom I've never had the opportunity to work with until now."

Gwendolyn lowered her head and humbly responded, "Yes, ma'am. Ms. Ilya, can I tell you something?"

Ilya placed the empty clothing bin back in its assigned storage space and then finally answered, "Of course."

Gwendolyn took a moment before proceeding. "I don't really want to go. I'm scared if I do all of the things they have in my plan and my father doesn't do right, I'm going to be stuck in DCFS custody for a long time. Honestly, I know I don't show it, but some of you staff members are like my family. Some of you guys are like my aunts and uncles," Gwendolyn went on to explain.

Ilya was floored by Gwendolyn's forthrightness and comfortability to be vulnerable in this defining moment. Although Gwendolyn had been on her best behavior the past weeks, she had never opened up and shared her feelings with staff the three years she had been back and forth to Barrington Hospital. The only emotion she had exhibited had been anger, and the behavior she displayed was mostly manipulation of the treatment team.

"Well, Gwendolyn, you have come a long way in such a short amount of time. I must reiterate once more about you having the ability to make healthy decisions the entire time in spite of your anger. I want you to think about this when you're feeling overwhelmed or vulnerable. If you want a different outcome to what you have been receiving, you have to do something different. Doing the same thing and expecting a different result is the definition of insanity." Gwendolyn smiled. "Young lady, do something different. What you've done to this point has obviously not worked for you." Gwendolyn mulled over Ilya's words of wisdom, and she stood up to hug Ilya. "That does make a lot of sense," Gwendolyn whispered.

It had been two weeks now since Gwendolyn returned to her placement after being discharged from Barrington Hospital. She was scheduled to be officially stepped down from her current placement into the independent living program under the guidance of her caseworker, who was assisted by a field worker contracted by DCFS to monitor young adults while in the independent living program. Things were going well for Gwendolyn, the overall plan seemed to be falling into place, and she had been compliant upon her return ever since the staffing meeting when the plan was introduced.

Gwendolyn was very nervous as she sat on the radiator in the hallway corridor waiting for her caseworker Bettye to arrive. Her father had been released from the correction facility weeks ago, and today she would meet him and her grandmother, along with the entire family on her father's side.

Gwendolyn couldn't help but feel accomplished that everything she had done the past couple of months had led her to this very moment. She saw Bettye's car driving up to the front of the residential. She couldn't believe this moment was happening. She was ecstatic she was finally getting a chance to meet her father and her family, but she had mixed feelings about how to react to them. She really didn't know them, and this caused a tremendous amount of anxiety for her.

"Good morning, young lady. Are you all set to go meet your family?" Bettye asked.

Gwendolyn forced a smile and answered, "Yes."

Bettye could see the uneasiness in Gwendolyn's body language and that her response was superficial. All the way to the Schultz Forest Preserve, Bettye constantly talked to Gwendolyn, but the girl was so engulfed in her own thoughts that the things Bettye said sounded like muffled background noise.

As they pulled into the Forest Preserve, Gwendolyn began to hear the music, saw smoke coming from barbecue grills, and now she could see people dancing and playing softball. Once she took in the scene, a smile came across her face. She had always wanted to be a part of family gatherings like this. She'd seen similar events on television, but now she was about to be a part of such an activity with her family.

When Bettye settled on the closest parking space to the walkway, they noticed three teenage girls running toward the car. Bettye was somewhat alarmed, but Gwendolyn continued smiling.

"You must be my cousin Gwendolyn. I'm your cousin Jasmine. Come meet the rest of the family, and Great Grandma Beatrice wants you to come to her first." Gwendolyn unbuckled her seatbelt and exited the car, running off with her cousins.

Bettye quickly got out of the car, locked her doors, and walked in the direction Gwendolyn had run with the other girls. She was staggered by Gwendolyn's sudden change of heart after being apprehensive prior to their arrival.

Stacey, another cousin, released Gwendolyn's hand and introduced her. "This is your Great Grandmother Beatrice. This is your father's, my great uncle's, grandmother. She is the matriarch of the family." Beatrice extended her hand to Gwendolyn with a tremendous smile on her face. Gwendolyn grabbed Beatrice's hand and stooped down to her knees in a sitting position.

"So, you're the missing piece to this family puzzle. I am so happy to meet you. I don't know how my grandson and this family allowed you to be away from us, but I hope you are here to stay."

Gwendolyn cried and rose to hug her great grandmother.

"I'm your uncle Elgin. Your father is my brother. These are my three daughters, Stephanie, Shantel, and Stacey, and this is my wife, Sadie. Welcome to the family, and welcome home."

Elgin embraced Gwendolyn as well, and many other family members began to gather and introduce themselves to Gwendolyn. After what went on for like twenty-five minutes of introductions and answering questions, Gwendolyn began to scan the park looking for her father.

"If you're looking for your father, he went to get your grandmother mother from the assisted living home. He should be back shortly. He was here early barbecuing the ribs and chicken. Are you hungry?" Sadie asked.

"Yes, ma'am, actually I am," Gwendolyn said.

"Come here, baby. I'll make you something to eat. My name is Margaret. I'm your father's first cousin. Betty-Jean is my mother. Gwendolyn continued smiling, not really knowing who Betty-Jean was. Her caseworker Bettye stood off to the side watching the meet and greet. Before walking off with her three cousins and Margaret, Gwendolyn noticed Bettye standing off to the side, and she asked, "Can my caseworker Ms. Wells have something to eat too? She brought me here, and she'll be driving me back."

Many of the family members turned to look at Bettye in the direction Gwendolyn was pointing.

"Oh, absolutely, you come right over and have your fill with Gwendolyn. We thank you so much for bringing her here today. I hope she doesn't have to leave early?" Margaret asked, as they all walked toward the picnic tables.

"As long as there is daylight, we are here. I set this day aside so she could come be with her family. I am off today, but I wanted very much for Gwendolyn to be here. She's worked so hard to get to this day," Bettye said.

They sat at a table, and Margaret went to the area where the food was to make Gwendolyn's and Bettye's plates. "I hope you girls aren't expecting me to make your plates. As a matter of fact, Shantel, come over here and help me," Margaret screeched at the younger cousins. Shantel wanted to remain at the table and get to know her cousin Gwendolyn, but she adhered to her aunt's request out of respect.

Gwendolyn was ecstatic to have conversation with her cousins. Talking with them, she realized even more how different her life was from theirs. Her cousins were able to attend regular schools, and they had friends near their homes in their neighborhoods. She basked in all of the attention she was getting, which before today she had craved but had to act out behaviorally in order to get it.

"Here come your father and your grandmother now," Margaret said. Gwendolyn turned to see her father pushing her grandmother in a wheelchair on the paved walkway. As they inched closer, her interest was piqued to know who the girl was that was walking alongside them. Once Percy made it to the picnic tables, without saying a word he opened his arms wide and walked toward Gwendolyn.

They embraced and held each other for an extended amount of time. Gwendolyn cried while most of the family surrounded them.

"I am so happy this day has finally come. I haven't laid eyes on you, baby, since you were two months old." He released Gwendolyn and kissed her on her forehead. "I have two people I want you to meet. This is your grandmother, Flora." Gwendolyn reached down to hug her grandmother, but Flora stood up, using the armrest on her wheelchair.

She hugged her granddaughter and whispered in her ear, "I am honored to meet you. I have always loved you, and we have a lot to catch up on."

After helping his mother safely sit back down in her wheelchair, Percy reached around to grab the hand of the young lady with him. "This is your sister, Maya, and Maya, this is your sister, Gwendolyn. You girls are nineteen months apart, and for the first time in our lives, we are all together."

The entire family began to clap and whistle in celebration of the historical family moment. Still and all while everyone was smiling and celebrating, Gwendolyn was stunned to learn she had a sister.

"I'm so glad to finally meet my one and only sister. I have three brothers from my mom's side, of course, but I've always wanted to have the opportunity to bond with my younger sister," Maya said.

They cleared a space for Flora at the end of the picnic table so that she could be comfortable in her wheelchair. Percy and Maya sat on each side of Gwendolyn at the table across from Stacey, Shantel, and Stephanie.

"So, are your foster parents okay with you having company and a relationship with your family? I really want us to connect with one another. I love my brothers, but I've always wanted to be able to do things with my sister," Maya said with eagerness.

"I haven't lived with my foster family for a few years now. I've been living in a residential for a year-and-a-half. Prior to that I was in a group home, and next week I'm going to be in an independent living program. I'll be sharing an apartment with another girl close to my age."

Maya looked confused and asked, "What's an independent living program?"

Bettye Wells had seen Gwendolyn's demeanor change the moment Percy had introduced Maya as his daughter. She decided to answer Maya's question, not wanting Gwendolyn to be overwhelmed with everything she was absorbing in this moment. "The independent living program services youth aging out-of-home care, as well as tools and strategies for improving transitions to adulthood. Gwendolyn has done all the necessary things that have put her in the position to be embarking upon this program." When Bettye spoke, many of Gwendolyn's family members couldn't understand why she was talking, because they didn't understand Gwendolyn's triggers.

"Tell those kids to change that music. It's working on my nerves. I don't know what they're saying, and I don't like the language in it," Flora said with frustration, drawing attention.

"Grandma, it's called hip hop. Why is it we can't listen to the kind of music we want to listen to? When we were kids, we had to listen to old folks' music," said Reginald, who was Margaret's son.

"I don't care what it's called, and who made this spaghetti? It's seasoned too high. I can feel my blood pressure rising by the second."

"I think your pressure is rising because you are yelling," Reginald retorted.

Flora turned to Percy and yelled, "Take me back home. Where I live at, I don't have to be bothered with all this noise, and most certainly not the disrespect. It's a shame I'm treated better at a facility than I am here amongst my own family."

Margaret motioned for her son to turn the music off, and he was very displeased. "Mom, we just got here a little while ago," Percy tried to explain. "This is the first time we can all be together as a family. They're changing the music now."

"I don't care. I want to go back home."

Percy didn't know what to do. He wanted to honor his mother, but he wanted to spend this time getting to know his daughter. He turned to Gwendolyn and said, "Let me take my mom back to the facility. She's only twenty-five minutes away. I promise when I get back, we'll have the rest of the day to talk, okay?"

Gwendolyn was trying to be understanding, but she didn't want her father to leave. She felt like it was her time and that she deserved his full attention. "Dad, while you're taking Grandma back to the nursing home, can you stop at the house on the way back and pick up my Adidas jacket on the bed in my room?" Maya asked.

"Wait, you live with him?" Gwendolyn asked her sister.

"Yes, the past couple of weeks. My uncle got us both jobs working at Loyola Hospital. We're going to share the rent, and this gives me an opportunity to spend some time with my dad. You can come stay with us anytime you want," Maya stated with ingenuous intent, not understanding the impact of her words.

Gwendolyn turned to her father. "I've been without my father all of my life. I didn't have a mother like she has, because my mother is dead," she yelled, and then took a deep breath.

"You told me when you got out you would be staying with your sister until you got on your feet. It sounds like you're on your feet, while I've been moved around from foster homes and placements. Immediately you get a job, a place to live, and you choose to live with a sister I didn't know I had?"

"Calm down, Gwendolyn," Bettye whispered.

"I don't want to calm down. I want him to answer my damn question." Everyone was attentive to what was going on at this point, and many were bewildered as to what was happening.

"I just started working days ago. I haven't gotten my first paycheck yet. I'm sleeping on an air mattress my sister gave me. I got the apartment and the job because Maya's uncle works for the alderman and he pulled some strings. Maya coming to live with me was not planned, and I shouldn't have to apologize for that."

Gwendolyn smiled before going into a rage. She slapped a cup of grape juice that splattered on different family members in close range. She pushed over the popcorn machine, shattering the glass, then walked away from the sitting area at the forest preserve with clenched fists.

"If this is how she acts when she is disappointed, she needs to be in one of those places," Margaret said, while feverishly trying to minimize the grape juice stains on her blouse. Bettye apologized to the family and ran after Gwendolyn. When she noticed that Gwendolyn stopped by her car, she stopped running after her and just walked at a brisk pace.

"It's okay, Gwendolyn, this is your first meet. I'm sure you were overwhelmed by taking in so much at one time. We can take it one visit at a time," Bettye said, trying to de-escalate Gwendolyn, who was obviously upset.

"Take me to the hospital!" she demanded.

"You mean take you back to your placement? You know if you go to the hospital, that will forfeit the independent living program. Everything you've worked so hard for would be lost," Bettye explained.

"Either you take me to the hospital or I'm going to jump out into traffic and end it all."

Bettye knew from Gwendolyn's history she would follow through on her threat. She opened her passenger door for Gwendolyn and drove her back to Barrington Hospital. By the time Bettye and Gwendolyn went through the emergency room process, while waiting to be screened by a SASS worker to be readmitted back into the adolescent psychiatry department, it was ten forty-five. Bettye had spent her entire day off to facilitate this meet and greet with Gwendolyn's family, and she was exhausted.

"I'm going to take off now. Assessment and referral will escort you to the unit. I'll come visit you Monday after I'm done with my caseload," Bettye said.

"Ms. Wells, I'm sorry I didn't handle it well. I just lost it when I found out Percy had that girl who is supposed to be my sister living with him. He didn't even think about me, Ms. Wells. I feel like after all I've been through, he should have thought of me first. But I am sorry, I know what I did earlier affects everything you've done to get me to this day. I just can't control myself when I get angry like that."

Bettye refrained from elaborating on what Gwendolyn said, because she knew she wouldn't receive it well, not to mention she herself was drained from this long admission process. "I'll see you Monday, and we'll form a new plan for the next chapter."

Eight days later the Dodd family were gathering for Sunday dinner at Beatrice Dodd's house. The family having Sunday dinner together had been a longstanding tradition. It was also a purposeful way to make sure the younger generations remained connected to Beatrice, the oldest living person in the family. It was important that they learned their history and about family tradition.

Elgin, who was Percy's brother, had some unfavorable news to report after Beatrice asked about her grandson Percy, who had been released from jail after fifteen years. "Well, where is that boy, and why isn't he here with us all?" Beatrice questioned.

The dining room connected to the living room was extremely quiet after her question. The family already knew the answer to Beatrice's question, but they were apprehensive about how the matriarch of the family would receive it. "Grandma Beatrice, Percy violated his parole, and he was arrested earlier this week when he visited his parole officer," Elgin said.

There was an awkward silence in the house for several moments as the family waited on the ninety-one-year-old elder statesman to speak. Both connected rooms were large, and there were many tables to accommodate all the family members that attended and the assigned dishes they had brought with them. Beatrice shook her head with disappointment but still offered no words. Finally, she uttered, "I guess the four walls of those facilities my daughter, grandson, and great-granddaughter have come to reside in have become familiar to them. My heart is broken that this boy has been away from his child all her life, and he's spent half his life locked up in that jail." Beatrice paused for a split second before speaking again. "I suspect family has become a low priority when people take comfort in being institutionalized."

THE ISSUE OF PEER PRESSURE

CHAPTER 5

PAULETTE LAY IN HER bed thinking about the plans for her eighteenth birthday she was to celebrate later this evening. Some of her friends that she had known since she was in grade school had planned a party to celebrate her birthday with some neighborhood friends, former classmates, and some of her current coworkers.

Paulette was extremely intelligent, and she graduated high school a year before her two best friends, Gilisa and Marilyn. While in middle school, Paulette had excelled in her academics so well the school had allowed her to skip seventh grade, placing her in eighth grade after her sixth-grade spring semester. Paulette, Gilisa, and Marilyn made a pact to all attend Loyola University. Against her parents' advice, Paulette decided to take a year off before attending Loyola to work and save money while she waited on her two friends to graduate.

As approved by her supervisor, Paulette was scheduled off from work today. Paulette currently worked at the Target in Broadview Square Mall. Her work ethic was similar to her principled academic abilities. She rose from her bed and stood in front of the mirror as though she was looking to see a change in her appearance because it was her birthday. She ran her hands across her face, stretching her skin, and then she maneuvered her fingers through her hair like a comb. Paulette had an appointment to get her hair styled at Melanin Hair Salon and now that she looked at the condition of her nails in the mirror while stretching the skin on her face, she planned to get her nails done as well. Paulette showered and put on a comfortable jogging outfit she rarely had the opportunity to wear because of her work schedule. She grabbed her keys and cell phone before exiting her bedroom, planning to grab a piece of toast before leaving the house.

The moment she opened her bedroom door, she could smell bacon that permeated the entire second floor. On her way downstairs, the smell of bacon became even more profound, but now she also detected the smell of bell peppers and onions. She walked into the kitchen, and her family was sitting at the kitchen table. "One, two, three, go," her mother, Marcine, chanted. The entire family began to sing Happy Birthday to her all at once.

After they sang, they each gave her a hug and a kiss. Her father, James, pulled out the chair that was next to him. "Come sit next to your father and have breakfast. You may be eighteen today, but you will always be my little girl."

Paulette smiled, knowing her father was always sincere with his words. Although she was the oldest of her siblings, her father maintained the same bond with her established from birth. Even still, she had a brother, Reginald, who was two years younger than her, and her baby sister, Janice, who was thirteen years of age. "I didn't get a hug and kiss from you," Paulette said to Reginald.

"I said Happy Birthday to you. I'm not doing all that sentimental stuff. I'm not one of your little boyfriends."

Marcine walked over and set a huge plate filled with two ham-and-cheese omelets, a large quantity of bacon with hash browns, and a waffle in front of Paulette. She kissed her daughter on both of her cheeks. "Enjoy, my lovely daughter, and this is nothing compared to the food I will be cooking for you tonight."

Paulette looked at her plate, knowing she wasn't going to eat even a third of what her mother had prepared for her. "Mom, you didn't have to cook all of this food. Why did you go to all this trouble for me? I was just going to have a piece of toast, pick up a cup of coffee, and stop at the bank before my hair appointment." Marcine touched her daughter's shoulder and simply announced, "Eat up. It's your birthday. You have time."

Paulette didn't challenge her mother, although she had no intention of consuming the amount of food that was on her plate. Besides that, she had a bigger dilemma than the food on her plate. Her friends had already made plans to celebrate her birthday, and it was news to her that her family had already planned a birthday dinner. Paulette began to work on her waffle, with her father periodically looking over at her and just smiling.

"Can I go with you to get your hair and nails done?" Janice asked.

"How are you going to go with me? You have school today." James looked over at Janice after Paulette asked her the question.

"We just have half a day today. The grades for the semester are coming out tomorrow. Today is just a show-up-for-attendance day. All the work has been done and the grades are already in."

"I don't mind you tagging along, but do you have money to get either your hair or nails done? And you better ask Dad is it okay for you to skip the half of a day."

"I have money to get my nails done. I don't need to get my hair done. I just want to hang out with my big sister."

As soon as Janice looked over at her father to ask could she stay home from school, he said before she could ask, "Ask your mother." Reginald snickered while drinking his orange juice. That was the same answer his father would give him when he didn't want to say no.

"It's fine with me. You've always maintained honor roll status. I can extend the rope a little further," Marcine said, while setting a freshly brewed cup of coffee in front of Paulette. Unexpectedly, there was a knock at the back door. James immediately rose from his seat and moved to the side of the door as he peaked around the door's wooden blinds.

When he saw that it was Gilisa and Marilyn, he immediately opened the door.

"Good morning, Mr. Barnes. I'm sorry to interrupt your breakfast, but can we speak to Paulette for a moment?" Gilisa asked humbly.

"Come inside and stop behaving as though you two are strangers here. You guys spent so much time here when you were in middle school, I should've been able to file you both on my taxes. Everyone in the kitchen laughed as Marilyn and Gilisa entered the kitchen, but Paulette was more inquisitive as to their unannounced presence.

"What are you guys doing here?" she asked with a smile on her face.

"We know you're going to the shop to get your hair done, so we thought we'd pick you up and start your birthday off on the right foot before your bash tonight," Marilyn said, naïve to the repercussions of her statement.

"You're not going to be here tonight for your dinner party? Your Aunt

Rochelle and your cousins were coming as a surprise to you," Marcine said.

Once again, Reginald snickered, enjoying every minute of the controversy. He already knew Paulette had issues with the way their Aunt Rochelle related everything about life to God. She especially took exception that her two cousins who were around her age had begun to do so as well. It ultimately put distance between their relationship.

"May I ask what time the dinner party is scheduled to begin?" Marilyn inquired.

"We're supposed to have dinner at six-thirty," Marcine said with discontent.

"Well, Paulette, what we planned for you doesn't start until nine. There's no reason why you can't do both," Marilyn said.

Paulette nodded, agreeing with Marilyn's assessment. She felt obligated to attend this dinner party she had no knowledge of. Nevertheless, she felt because it was her birthday, she should be able to do what she wanted without the onus being placed on her to choose between what others had planned.

"Seems like the problem is solved," Paulette's father said. "Go on and take care of your business, young lady, and thank you, Marilyn, for your quick resolution."

"Oh, no problem, Mr. Barnes. I'm glad it worked out for everyone. Come on, ladies, we better get going if we're going to look our best for tonight."

Marcine walked back to the stove to discard the rest of the batter mix of the waffles. She was dismayed by the fact that Paulette had to struggle to choose between her friends' plans and the plans the family had made to celebrate her birthday. Marcine was a believer of Christ: she made sure her children were exposed to the beliefs and lifestyles that came along with being a Christian, but they were older now, especially Paulette. Exposure to what was common in the new millennium among her friends and the younger generation of society caused Paulette to minimize the relevancy of having a relationship with God.

Just as Paulette and her friends were exiting the kitchen, Janice yelled, "Hey, I'm still going, right? I want to get my nails done too."

Paulette was entangled with everything that had happened since she left her bedroom. Her entire day had been altered from what she had thought it would be. She'd already committed to letting Janice accompany her, prior to her friends arriving.

"Do you mind if Janice comes with us? I told her she could ride with me before you guys arrived." Janice sat waiting for a response.

"Sure, if she's okay with sitting after her nails are done, and if she doesn't mind tagging along for my other errands," Gilisa answered.

Paulette didn't like the sound of that, and she didn't want to be on Gilisa's time on her birthday, so she responded, "I'll just drive my car, and we'll meet you guys at the shop." Janice was elated. She really wanted to ask her father for money to have her hair styled as well, but since she had already received the green light to opt out of attending school, she didn't want to press the issue with him, especially since it was really Paulette's day.

The girls left the house, and although James was pleased by the compromise, he knew his wife was discontented about having to share their daughter's day with Paulette's friends. Marcine had already purchased all of Paulette's favorite foods, and she would be in the kitchen most of the day preparing dinner. In addition, she still had to prepare the house for guests, and find the perfect outfit for the occasion.

When Paulette and Janice pulled up in front of Melanin Hair Salon, Marilyn and Gilisa had already parked and were standing outside next door to the salon talking to a man and a woman. As the two approached from Paulette's car, Marilyn said, "They have Ardell Natural Eyelashes for ten dollars. They cost forty-five at the beauty supply store." Paulette walked over to view the different selections of eyelashes the man and woman were selling.

"If you guys make a purchase, we don't take cash. We've been burned too many times with counterfeit money. We only take credit and debit cards," the man, named Pharell, explained, while the girls continued looking through the selection of eyelashes the woman displayed.

"Are you guys really about to buy some fake eyelashes from some people you don't even know, right out here on the street using your debit cards? How gullible can you guys be? It's obviously a scam," Janice said emphatically.

"Cute, kid, it's obvious you're not into fashion yet, because anybody that is anybody knows that Ardell Natural Eyelashes are just what they claim to be. Natural eyelashes." The woman quickly closed her case. "Fine then, go buy those fake eyelashes at international prices from those Koreans up the street."

Gilisa was heated. "I knew this was a bad idea to let your baby sister tag along."

Janice chimed in, "That doesn't make any sense. How are you going to call the eyelashes the Koreans sell fake when they're all fake eyelashes? It says so right on the front of the box."

"Paulette, if your sister has to be with us today, can you please control her mouth?" Gilisa said in frustration.

Before Janice could respond, Paulette steered her toward the hair salon. "Can you just go inside, please? We'll be there in a moment."

The girls each made their purchases and entered Melanin Beauty Salon, where Janice was already receiving service by a nail technician by the name of Carmen. When the girls entered the salon, many of the patrons and hair stylists were gawking at the television, watching the first interview of Michelle Obama's twelve-stop book tour with Oprah Winfrey. It appeared as if there was more television watching going on in this place of business than actual service, as the hairstylists' eyes remained glued to the television.

After standing by the check-in desk for several moments, Gilisa finally spoke out. "Is anyone working today? We have appointments, and my friend doesn't want to spend all of her birthday in this shop."

"Shhh," Karen, one of the hairstylists and owner of Melanin Beauty Salon, said in the girls' direction, then directed her attention back to the interview.

Kara, one of the two shampoo girls who worked in the salon, walked over to the service desk and apologized to Paulette, Gilisa, and Marilyn while handing each of them a bottle of water. "I'm so sorry ladies, this interview was last night, and Karen recorded it on the DVR so she could watch it with the clients that haven't had the opportunity to watch it. I'll be getting each one of you ladies started with Brenda, the other preparation tech. Do you ladies know whether you'll be having deep conditioner or systematic conditioner?" Kara caught the stares of several women in the shop who were finding it difficult to hear Michelle answering Oprah's questions.

Gilisa needed her braids to be taken down before she began receiving her washout and conditioner. Kara took care of her while Brenda serviced Paulette and Gilisa by washing their hair.

The interview went to commercials, and Karen seized the break to acknowledge Paulette and her friends. "I'm sorry, ladies, we were a bit caught up with our former first lady. I heard one of you ladies say that it was your birthday?"

"It's her birthday," Marilyn answered and pointed toward Paulette. Karen walked over to Paulette while her head was bent back into the wash bowl. She touched her leg and said, "Happy Birthday, sweetie. Show Brenda your I.D. to confirm your birthday, and we'll give you twenty-five percent off your hairstyle."

Paulette said, "Thank you," her words echoing from inside the wash bowl.

"How old are you today?" Brenda asked Paulette while massaging her scalp.

"I'm eighteen today. So, I guess you can say I'm officially legal," Paulette responded with poise.

"Don't be in such a rush to be a legal adult. Believe me, it's not all it's cracked up to be. Do you have plans for this evening?"

Paulette paused before answering. "Yes, but I don't know exactly what the evening will entail with my friends. Not knowing is kind of making the evening mysterious, yet exciting at the same time. Even still, I have a boring dinner obligation with my family. It's great that they're thinking of me, but I feel like this is my birthday and I should be able to celebrate it the way I want."

Brenda added more shampoo to Paulette's hair and continued to massage her scalp. "You're right, but to have a family that wants to celebrate you and shower you with love on your birthday is not the worst thing in the world. I only wish my mom was still here to celebrate and spend time with. I'm an only child, and my father has Alzheimer's."

"When you say it like that, it makes me feel guilty. I love my family. I know I'm lucky to have my family, but my mother can be too religious sometimes. She's inviting my aunt and my two cousins, and everything they do they have to say if it's the Lord's will, or to God be the Glory. They act as though they're not in control of anything they do. My two cousins, who I was very close with growing up, behave as though they're brainwashed now. No teenagers I know talk like them. They wear skirts instead of leggings, and they wear stockings whenever they wear dresses. My grandmother is the only person I know that still wears stockings with a skirt." Brenda and everyone within earshot of Paulette's comments began to laugh.

Suddenly the door chime of the shop sounded, alerting that someone was entering the front door. It was the same man and woman who had been outside of the salon selling eyelashes. By this time Paulette was sitting under the dryer, while Brenda was washing Marilyn's hair. Karen, the shop owner, paused the interview after noticing the man and woman entered the salon. "The two of you can turn right around and leave my place of business."

Janice was done getting her nails done, but she was now having her eyebrows arched. She paid special attention to what Karen was saying, although she couldn't see her while leaned back in the chair by the technician.

"Ma'am, we are not trying to interrupt your place of business, but can you explain to these ladies that these are the finest Ardell eyelashes you can purchase?" the woman said, pointing in the direction of Gilisa and Paulette.

But before either of them could respond, Karen sounded off once again. "I don't give a damn about your eyelashes. I'm well aware that portable debit card machine is a way to copy people's debit cards so you can steal their identity. Now please get out of my salon before I call the police."

They both turned to leave the shop without further objection.

"Are you sure they are stealing people's identity?" Paulette asked.

"Don't tell me you girls used your cards to buy those fake eyelashes from those people?"

At this time Janice was sitting up and no longer leaning back while her eyebrows were being arched. "Why does everyone keep saying fake eyelashes, like they sell real eyelashes. They're all fake." No one responded to Janice's statement of frustration.

"You girls might want to call your banking institutions immediately," Karen instructed.

Paulette and Marilyn called their respective banks to put a stop on their debit cards, but the customer service operators couldn't tell them whether any transactions had been made on their cards, due to the fact their system was down and the banks were doing everything manually. Gilisa only had enough money on her to get her hair and nails done, so Marilyn paid for her eyelashes, with the intent that Gilisa would reimburse her.

After getting their hair done and being serviced by the shop's nail technicians, the girls left the salon. Almost immediately Paulette could see from the front of the salon that her car was gone.

"Didn't you park your car in front of the cell phone shop?" Janice asked.

Paulette ignored her younger sister, and at this very moment, more than any other time today, she wished she'd left her at home. Paulette reached into her handbag to obtain her cell phone and dialed 911. The police came, and Paulette made a police report about her car and her debit card. She assumed the man and woman selling the eyelashes were probably responsible for stealing her car as well. They saw where she parked, and they knew she would be in the hair salon for a long time. She reached into her handbag once more to locate the entry remote to her car, but it wasn't there. Paulette couldn't help but feel that she had been victimized on her birthday.

"Well, there isn't anything you can do about it now. Don't cry over spilled milk. Just enjoy the rest of your birthday," Janice said.

Gilisa looked over at Janice with disdain. She felt Janice had too much to say for someone she didn't want to accompany them from the very beginning.

"What do you want to do, Paulette?" Marilyn asked. "I need for you to drive me to my house so Janice can be dropped off, and I really need to go by my job to pick up a birthday card and some money. My coworker

Maria took up a collection for my birthday."

"Absolutely. But right after that, I need to pick my mom up from work, and then we'll have the rest of the evening to ourselves. I promise the party tonight will take your mind off your car being stolen," Marilyn said encouragingly. In fact, Marilyn didn't really need to pick her mother up from her job. This was part of the surprise the girls hadn't communicated, that they'd take Paulette to the lounge Marilyn's aunt owned. Paulette had never drunk alcohol before, and Marilyn had already set it up with her aunt to have a room off to the side of the lounge where they would each be served a limit of two drinks to celebrate Paulette's birthday.

Janice didn't want to be driven home. Like her mother, she felt Paulette was choosing what her friends wanted over what she wanted, which was to spend the day with her older sister. Upon arrival at their home, Janice exited the car without saying a word.

At the next stop, Paulette asked in confusion, "Why are we stopping here. I thought we had to pick your mother up at work and drive her to your house?"

"You know she's not going to go inside. I don't know why you thought it would be a good idea to bring her here," Gilisa said negatively.

"What's going on. Why are we at your aunt's lounge?"

Marilyn turned around to face Paulette, who was in the rear seat of her car. "My Aunt Deborah is going to take care of us. It's still the afternoon. Not many people will be in there, and we have a little private room off to the side of the lounge. Let's set your birthday off right as you embark upon adulthood," Marilyn said, trying to sound convincing.

"You were supposed to take me to pick up the birthday money my co-workers collected for me."

"When we leave here, I have to take you to your house for your birthday dinner. Target is along the way. I haven't forgotten," Marilyn said.

Paulette thought about it for a moment and surprisingly responded, "Okay, let's do it."

They went inside the lounge, and Marilyn's Aunt Deborah was talking to a couple of patrons at a table. The lights were dim, and there was soft soul music playing in the background.

"Boy, this place is dead. Old people always act as though they have it going on. There are like five people in here, and the vibe is turned all the way down. I thought we were going to turn it up," Gilisa said.

As soon as Deborah saw Marilyn and her two friends, she quickly scampered the girls off to the private room at the rear of the lounge. "You know I could get into a lot of trouble for having minors in my place of business," Deborah stated seriously.

"We know, Aunt Deborah. I've already told my friends about the situation. We really appreciate you doing this for us," Marilyn said.

"You must be Paulette, because I've met Gilisa before," Deborah asked.

"Yes, I'm Paulette. Nice to meet you, ma'am."

Deborah frowned and then responded. "Let's do away with the ma'am stuff. Everyone calls me Debbie. But if it makes you feel comfortable, you can call me Ms. Lucas. Oh, and happy birthday to you. I speak peace and prosperity into your life. Your first drink is on the house. You all are limited to two drinks. Oh, and Marilyn, you will be leaving your car here with me. You guys can take an Uber back home."

Paulette was stunned to hear that.

"Something wrong?" Debbie asked. "You guys better make up your minds real fast, because if you're drinking, you're not driving." She quickly exited the room to greet the two people that entered her lounge.

"Well, what's it going to be?" Gilisa asked.

"We'll have the drinks and take an Uber to Paulette's house for the dinner party with her folks. We'll be there a couple of hours. The alcohol will have subsided, and we can swing back to get the car, get dressed, and get to the real party."

Debbie walked back in and opened her hands to receive Marilyn's keys without discussion. "Now, what will you girls be having tonight?" Paulette looked over at Marilyn, indicating she didn't know what to order.

"Aunt Debbie, can we see a menu or something? It's not like we do this kind of thing all the time," Marilyn asked respectfully.

"Well, this isn't a restaurant. Okay, I'll make some suggestions for you ladies to choose from. How does that sound?"

"Thank you, Ms. Lucas. I've never drunk alcohol before, and I honestly do not know what to order," Paulette said.

Debbie smiled at Paulette's naïve statement. "I tell you what, I'm going to make you a pina colada. I'm sure you'll like it, and if you don't, I'll bring you something else."

Paulette, feeling like she didn't have much choice in the matter, responded, "Okay."

"Gilisa, what is it that you'll be having? Would you like a beer, a strawberry daiquiri, or a margarita?"

Gilisa answered without hesitation. "I'll have a rum and Coke, please."

Debbie was amused once again. "And what will you be having?"

Marilyn cleared her throat and said, "I'll have a margarita this round, and the next round I'll have the strawberry daiquiri."

Debbie wrote the order down on the small pad in her hand. "For someone that needed a menu, you ladies sound like regulars here. Nevertheless, when drinking, this is the rule. Whatever you start out drinking, that's what you finish up drinking. So, if you're having a margarita, that's what your next drink will be. Anything different and you'll have a long night. The last thing I need is for your mothers to be chastising me for having you crumb snatchers in here," Debbie said before leaving the private room for a second time.

Marilyn walked over to the exit door leading to the outside of the private room and opened it. She looked out as though she was looking for something or someone in particular. Paulette watched her, wondering what she was doing, but she didn't verbalize her curiosity.

Gilisa turned up the volume on the Bluetooth Bose speaker in the room after hearing a song she recognized. It was a song her parents played religiously at home. In that moment, two men walked through the door, and Marilyn quickly closed the door behind them.

"I want you guys to meet my very best friend, and today is her birthday. She's the reason we're all here today."

Paulette smiled and extended her hand to Cameron, whom she'd seen before at her mother's church when they were selling dinners on Saturday to raise money for the Temple Project.

"Don't I know you?" Cameron asked, not letting go of Paulette's hand.

"Well, I wouldn't say you know me, but if I'm not mistaken, you make food deliveries for Wesleyan Ministry, right?"

Cameron paused for a second, then said, "Yes, that's where I recognize you from. I may forget places and situations, but believe me when I tell you, I can never forget a face as gorgeous as yours."

Gilisa laughed aloud and then said, "This guy is laying it on kind of thick, and he hasn't been here sixty seconds."

Cameron released Paulette's hand and stepped to the side to introduce his friend Ryan. "This is my guy Ryan. He attends Fenwick High School, and he plays varsity football for the school."

Paulette shook Ryan's hand, but she was still a bit puzzled about what was taking place. She looked over at Gilisa, who simply shrugged her shoulders.

"It's nice to meet you, Paulette, and Happy Birthday," Ryan said sincerely.

"Thank you," Paulette said. "Where are you from? I hope this doesn't sound rude, but I love the way you enunciate every single syllable. I'm so used to people our age frowning upon using proper English as though it's some sort of crime."

Ryan smiled, but before he could answer, Debbie walked back into the room with the drinks the girls ordered.

"I see you've completely made yourself comfortable and added more people to this unauthorized party. It would have been nice if you would have told me it was going to be five people instead of three." Marilyn was prepared to respond, but Debbie continued: "The same rule applies for them as you girls, that is, a maximum of two drinks. I know they must be illegal too. It goes without saying that they're paying for their own drinks. How are you boys doing?" Ryan and Cameron each spoke to Debbie in a respectful manner.

"What are you boys drinking?" Debbie asked, without making eye contact with either of them. She instead pulled her pad and pencil out of the waist pouch of her apron she used to take orders and collect money until she placed the money and receipts into the cash register.

"I'll have a Heineken beer," Cameron answered confidently.

Ryan answered accordingly. "I'll take a Corona with lime if you have it."

Debbie checked off a box on her pad for beer. "You boys ever heard of domestic beer? You know, beer that's made here in the good ole United States of America, and Marilyn, please explain to your little friend that we do have lime. This is a lounge, for Pete's sake. Little pissant, wet behind the ears. New millennial smart ass."

Gilisa laughed aloud for an extended period of time. Marilyn simply shook her head, feeling embarrassed by her aunt, but she dared not say anything, since her aunt was already stretching for her. Debbie would have been well within her rights if she had asked the boys to leave, due to the fact that Marilyn never mentioned anything about having male company.

"If you're going to compromise the security of my establishment by letting in strangers, you could at least lock up the way you found my door," Debbie stated with all seriousness.

"Aunt Debbie, I did lock the door," Marilyn affirmed.

"You most certainly did not. This bottom lock is not turned, and the deadbolt lock you attempted to lock is not all the way past the striker plate. You have to lift up on the door in order for it to securely lock inside the groove." Debbie set her waist pouch on a stool and lifted the door to turn the deadbolt securely.

"When you boys leave my lounge, please leave through the front door like everyone else." Debbie exited the room holding up two fingers while shouting, "Two drinks in two hours, and all of you are gone. This establishment is not a hangout for you juvenile delinquents."

Ryan walked over and sat next to Marilyn. He handed her two candy bars he knew she liked but not sold at every store.

"Thank you. You know I really like these, but not as much as I like you."

Gilisa rolled her eyes at Marilyn's statement. "I wish you would have told me that we were inviting other people, especially boys. I thought we were supposed to be celebrating Paulette's birthday together and just meet up with everyone including boys at the party tonight," Gilisa said purposely, knowing Marilyn hadn't invited Ryan to the party.

"Oh, so you guys are having a party tonight? I don't recall getting an invitation," Ryan said sarcastically.

"So, I don't see you at the church much anymore. I'm there on Saturdays and Sundays," Cameron said.

Paulette said, "Well, I work every other weekend, and when I'm off I kind of want to do the things that I want to do. I used to go to church with my mom every Sunday, and Thursday night for Bible class, but I really don't think you have to be at church every time the doors open or refer to God in every situation. I feel like my mom and other believers are overdoing it when it's not necessary."

Cameron looked over at Paulette somewhat puzzled. "Maybe they don't feel like they're overdoing it. Maybe they enjoy service and serving. Probably as much as you enjoy drinking and hanging out in bars."

Paulette was stunned by Cameron's comment, but he quickly laughed it off. "I'm just kidding with you. I'm not what you would call a Jesus freak. Seriously though, I don't pass judgment on people, but I feel like delivering church dinners on Saturday and going to a two-hour service on Sunday is the least I could do after Jesus made the ultimate sacrifice."

Paulette took a moment to process Cameron's statement. "I guess when you look at it that way, it puts some things in perspective. I shouldn't get distracted by what my mom or my aunt does or doesn't do. I just need to focus on what I should be doing."

Debbie walked into the private room, pushing the door with such force that the knob placed a small dent in the drywall. She set the two beers on the counter in the private room. "I left my receipts and my money pouch in here, and I see it's not on the bar stool where I set it when I locked the side door." The room was filled with silence as Debbie gave a direct stare to each individual one at a time.

"Are you sure you didn't leave with it, and possibly set it somewhere else in the lounge?" Marilyn asked.

Debbie stared at Marilyn, obviously irritated by her question. "I'm positive. I made the drinks, and when I went to take an order from another patron, I realized I didn't retrieve my pouch off this stool. Again, it has my money and receipts in it. Someone better come up with it by the time I come back or I'm calling the police," Debbie said before storming out of the room as forcefully as she had entered it.

Marilyn immediately began looking around the room to see if the pouch had fallen somewhere off the stool. "If someone has her pouch, please give it to her. I don't need for my birthday to take another left turn," Paulette added.

"I didn't see her put the pouch on the chair, but we didn't have any issues until we opened the door for other people to come in," Gilisa insinuated.

"How about you stop making snide remarks and help us look for the pouch? We don't need our parents to know we were even here," Marilyn said.

Debbie re-entered the private room. "I've already called the police. No one is leaving this room until the police get here. Jimmy is going to make sure of that." Jimmy was one of the mixologists who worked for Debbie. He was also a former nightclub bouncer. His arms and biceps were noticeably chiseled.

"If I give you your pouch, can I leave before the police get here?" Ryan asked.

Marilyn quickly turned around and faced Ryan. "You stole from my aunt while you're here asking to get to know me better?"

Jimmy walked past Debbie and over to Ryan. "This isn't a negotiation. Give me the pouch or you will be folded up before the cops get here.

You can give up the pouch, willingly or unwillingly."

Ryan thought about his options, and after sizing Jimmy up, he reached into the front pocket of his pants, pulled out the pouch, and handed it to Jimmy.

"I didn't know he did that. I'm with him, but I had no knowledge of this. I assure you ma'am, I didn't know he did this," Cameron explained to Debbie.

"I don't blame you. Your friend is the only person going to jail today. If there is anyone to blame, it's me for trusting my niece to be in my lounge in the first place. I don't know what I was thinking. I could lose my license for this. Just get out of my lounge before the police arrive." Ryan didn't need to be warned twice. Without hesitation he ran out of the bar.

"You're going to just let him off the hook after he came in here and stole from you?" Gilisa asked.

"I never called the police. I only said that because I knew if Jimmy took away the option to run, and I threatened to call the police, the culprit would definitely come forward. Besides, he's not getting away with anything. You better believe he'll try to steal again from someone else. Thieves always do, until they're caught. I'm holding myself accountable for what happened here as well. I'm calling each of your parents to tell them what I did."

Paulette was awestruck by Debbie's sudden stance of integrity. She had a little over an hour before she was due back home for her birthday celebration. She couldn't help but feel what started out as being an exciting, monumental birthday had settled into being a day of inconvenience and compromise. Her debit card and her vehicle were stolen, and now she knew she would have to explain why she was in a lounge drinking alcohol. She turned to Marilyn and stated, "Can you take me home? It's the least you could do, and I won't be attending that party later. From the moment I woke up this morning, I've been subjected to pressure from my family and my friends. I think my eighteenth birthday is the perfect time for me to stop following, and do what it is I want to do." Marilyn was disappointed, but she dared not question Paulette, knowing all of this was her idea to begin with.

THE ISSUE OF *un***FORGIVE**ness

CHAPTER 6

Marlene sat at the island counter in her kitchen on one of the stools eating aged Gouda cheese while sipping a glass of wine. She watched her daughter Stephanie periodically walk to the large picture window in the living room. Stephanie was waiting for her father, Daren, to pick her up for the weekend. She struggled to carry the heavy backpack filled with clothes and schoolbooks. Stephanie had assignments, and homework needed to completed over the weekend.

"Why is Dad always late? Every Friday I'm waiting, because he's never on time," Stephanie said out of frustration.

"It's probably because he's a jackass," Marlene mumbled to herself.

"What did you say, Mom?"

On cue Marlene responded to her daughter. "You know how your father is. From now on, don't be in a rush to get ready. The arrangement is for him to pick you up at five o'clock, so learn to expect him at about five-thirty." Stephanie heard her mother, but she didn't put much stock into what her mother was offering. Marlene walked over to her wine rack and put another bottle of Chardonnay wine in the freezer.

She had no plans for the weekend, and she'd just completed a fifty-two-hour work week, due to the Chicago Public Schools' being plagued by a shortage of Registered Nurses across the city. She had found herself covering more schools in her district this year, and she was also having to journey outside of the schools' district. Her day entailed a lot of driving that exceeded an eight-hour work day, and she still had plenty of paperwork to fill out for each school, which took another two to three hours. Marlene had been invited to attend one of her colleagues, Bethany's, spring party at her home, but Marlene had turned down the invitation and vowed to attend Bethany's next event. Marlene's plans for the weekend consisted of getting up early Saturday morning to aerate the soil for her rose garden. Her failed attempt to have a rose garden last year was due to lack of attention and educational know-how on planting, growing, and pruning. She committed to a lot of research over the winter, and she'd had several unauthorized consultations with the florist who worked for Jewel Osco.

After tending to her garden, Marlene planned to have brunch alone at Midway Café. She wouldn't have to cook breakfast for Stephanie, so she wanted to relax and treat herself. Afterwards, she planned to binge-watch a series on Netflix that she hadn't had time for.

"He's here, Mommy. Have a good weekend, and I'll call you tomorrow," Stephanie yelled as she ran over excitedly to hug and kiss her mother before exiting their house.

Marlene really loved spending time with her daughter on the alternative weekend when she wasn't with her father, but after the tiring work week, she was looking forward to solitude. Marlene walked over toward the window and watched her daughter climb into her father's Dodge Ram 1500 truck.

Marlene never communicated with Daren unless it was absolutely necessary concerning their daughter. Marlene walked over to the counter and poured herself another glass of wine, this time filling her glass to the rim. She then opened her iPad and opened her Kindle app to continue reading a book by the name of *When Justice isn't Just.*.

No sooner had she grabbed her wine and her iPad and headed toward the couch, than her cell phone rang. She didn't recognize the number, but she decided to answer anyway. "Hello," She answered with some hesitancy.

"Hey, baby, I'm so glad you answered. I left my cell phone at home because I was in such a rush. I'm actually using a pay phone at MacNeal Hospital," Marlene's mother, Alice, said frantically.

"Slow down, Mom. Why are you at the hospital? Are you all right?" Marlene asked after tossing her iPad on the couch and setting her glass of wine down on the cocktail table.

"It's not me. It's your father. He's been lying around the house for the past couple of days stating he wasn't feeling well, but I couldn't get him to go to the doctor. He fell in the bathroom due to dizziness, so I just called an ambulance." The anxiety Marlene was feeling decreased once she learned the issue was with her father, Fredrick, and not her mother.

"Can you come to the hospital? I don't know what's going on. They're running tests, but I know something's not right."

Marlene picked up her glass and took a sip, followed by a deep sigh, before saying, "Mommy, Fredrick will be fine. You know the relationship my father and I have. I just worked fifty-two hours this week. Plus, I've been drinking. I refuse to be irresponsible and be one of those individuals driving on the road while my coordination is altered. I'm already on my second glass of wine. Can you please call Reginald to come be with you?"

There was initially a moment of silence. "Your brother Reginald and his wife are already on their way. This is a time that all of the family should be together. This is not the time to focus on past grudges."

Marlene became quiet. She didn't offer any response to her mother.

"Are you still there?" Alice asked.

"Yes, I'm still here, Mom. Look, Mom, you know I love you and will do anything for you. But that doesn't extend to all things concerning my father. He severed ties with me a long time ago when he made a decision about my life that I'm reaping the consequences for."

"Marlene, that was over twenty years ago. Can't you find it in your heart to forgive him? We have to learn to forgive one another. We all have made mistakes," Alice pleaded.

"I know, Mom, and you're right, but I haven't been able to find peace with what my father did to me yet, and until I do, this is where I am in our relationship."

Alice was very upset with her daughter, but she knew there was no point in going further. She could hear the coldness in Marlene's voice, although Marlene had never verbalized any blame toward her. She knew her daughter harbored some underlying feelings toward her for allowing Fredrick to make a life altering decision when Marlene was seventeen. That decision her father made traumatized Marlene to this day.

"Bye, Mom, I'll check on you later," Marlene said before pushing the end button on her cell phone. She flopped down on her mahogany leather couch, relieved the hospital call wasn't about her mother's health. She opened her iPad and tapped the button on the screen asking her if she wanted to continue reading from where she had ended before going to bed last night.

She read only one paragraph before setting the iPad on the cocktail table, then taking two large swallows of wine from her glass. She was upset at herself for feeling guilty for not going to the hospital to see about her father, but most importantly to support her mother. She didn't like having these feelings for a man who had forced her to have an abortion when she was almost an adult. Marlene had become pregnant after being forced to have non-consensual sex with her best friend Kimberly's older brother, Teddy, who was four years older than her. Marlene had a crush on Teddy for years because he was charming and good-looking.

Even still, she wasn't sexually active at that time. One evening she came over looking for Kimberly, who'd gone to visit an aunt with her parents and younger brother. Teddy informed Marlene that Kimberly wasn't home but that she was welcome to come inside. Teddy knew that Marlene had a crush on him, because Kimberly had mentioned it to him several times over the years. "I have a frozen pizza in the oven, and I was just about to watch *Living Single*. Why don't you hang out for a little while? I'm sure they'll be back in no time." Flattered that Teddy wanted to spend time with her, Marlene entered the house without hesitation. She frequented their home regularly anyway, as did Kimberly often visit her home.

Teddy exited the living room to attend to cutting the pizza, but not before sharing his schoolbook photos that had a lot of pictures of him in his football uniform. Kimberly recognized many of the teachers who still taught at Manfred High School. She currently attended the same school with Kimberly. Teddy re-entered the living room with the pizza and two sodas under his arm.

“I didn’t know you had Mr. Partez. He’s my English teacher and my homeroom teacher,” Marlene said with excitement.

“Oh yeah, old Tez has been there since the first brick was laid at the school,” Teddy said jokingly. “He’s a good teacher, though. He saved my hide from getting cut from the squad quite a few times.”

Marlene was a little surprised Teddy was so forthcoming with her on this day. In times past, Teddy would speak in a dry manner to Marlene when she was visiting Kimberly, and he never had been interested in having a conversation with her before.

Marlene had two slices of the pizza before announcing she’d had enough. She leaned back on the couch, giving the indication she’d had her fill. She opened her soda can, and it made a loud sound of release of the trapped pressured air.

“This is one of very few shows that I will make the time to watch. This along with sports is about as much television as I watch,” Teddy explained.

“I love Sinclaire and Overton’s relationship. You can tell their attraction is both emotional and physical,” Marlene added.

Teddy placed the remaining plate of pizza he had in his hand on the table and slid back on the couch. He moved in closer to Marlene, then wrapped his arm around her. “That really sounds like something I would like to have with you.” Marlene was frozen, blindsided by Teddy’s forwardness, her feelings torn between feeling flattered and apprehensive of what was about to happen next. "I've been sweet on you for a while, but because of our age difference, I've fought back how I really feel about you. I'm at a place where I don't want to do that anymore. I think we should let love happen and not get focused on numbers."

Before Marlene could accurately process what was happening, Teddy invaded her personal space by grabbing the back of her head, pulling her closer. He then began kissing her passionately. Marlene didn't resist, overwhelmed with how fast this was happening. Teddy's pursuit didn't allow her time to think or feel comfortable with his advances. Due to the fact that Marlene never pulled away from him or stopped him, Teddy unwisely assumed the lack of resistance was Marlene's consent. He pushed her back on the couch with some aggression, and with both hands he pulled off her sweat pants and underwear at once. Marlene quickly closed her legs. She was exposed in a way she had never been exposed before. Marlene was a virgin, and although she couldn't constructively consent to what was happening, the reality remained that she really liked Teddy, and she didn't want to come off as a little girl to him in this passage-to-womanhood moment. Teddy climbed on top of her, leaning his weight on the upper portion of her body. He reached back with his right hand, and maneuvered his basketball shorts to his thighs. With no consideration of how she would feel, and with no form of affection, Teddy quickly entered Marlene. She screeched as he continued forcing his way in.

"Wait, it doesn't feel right," she gasped, trying to endure the pain his erect penis was causing.

"It feels right to me. Nothing could be more right," Teddy said as he lay on top of her, weighing his body against hers. His head was adjacent to hers, but faced downward toward the couch where she couldn't see his face. He continued to thrust wildly against her until he climaxed after a few minutes. He lay on her for another thirty seconds, grunting and gasping as evidence that all of his energy was expelled.

Marlene had moved past the point of the initial pain. Nevertheless, her facial expression was one of shock. She felt soiled after feeling the warmness of Teddy's release inside her. Teddy at last lifted himself from Marlene, and stood up over her. Marlene could visibly see his erection covered with sperm and her blood. Teddy pulled up his basketball shorts and gave Marlene a cold directive. "You can go to the bathroom right there to clean up. I'm going to the kitchen." Marlene looked down and saw moistness and blood on the couch. She felt misused and dirty. This definitely wasn't how she envisioned she would lose her virginity. She carefully maneuvered off the couch, trying not to smear the couch even further. She stepped into her underwear and sweat pants all in one motion. She then exited the front door of the house without uttering a single syllable.

Sometime after this traumatic experience, Marlene came to know she was pregnant. She told her parents, but she did not tell them that Teddy was the father. Marlene never even confided in Kimberly about being violated by her brother, and to the present day Marlene and Kimberly remained best friends.

Plagued with guilt, Marlene felt as though she had caused much of this and still possessed feelings of shame. In actuality Teddy was at fault, and the violation came with no remorse on his part. Two weeks after Marlene had told her parents, her father took her to an abortion clinic, to feticide the fetus growing inside her. Fredrick was more concerned about how this would be looked upon by his family, the community, and society altogether. He cared more about the family's image, more so than displaying the love and support his daughter needed. Marlene had managed to keep this dreadful secret to herself, but it hadn't come without a price. Her social life was limited, because she unconsciously isolated herself whenever she wasn't working.

Unable to deal with the feelings she was having at this moment, Marlene turned the light off in her living room and proceeded to her bedroom. She changed into her night clothing, buried her head under the comforter and forced herself to go to sleep. This was one of the ways Marlene avoided dealing with her unresolved issue. Her guilty feelings about not going to the hospital to support her mother on her father's behalf led her to having thoughts about the abortion her father had forced her to have.

She woke up the next morning at a little after six, which was customarily the time she would wake up to go to work on weekdays. Marlene went to the kitchen to get a bottle of water from her refrigerator, and then walked into the bathroom to brush her teeth after consuming the water.

Marlene had neglected to brush her teeth the previous night, which was a habitual routine before going to bed. Her mouth felt unclean, and she tried to remove the taste of wine from her mouth that had marinated overnight. After brushing her teeth for a second time, she hopped into the shower, dressed, and went directly to her garage. She obtained the supplies she'd purchased to prepare to sod the carved-out space below her bedroom window. She spent two hours working on the soil, and after squaring off a wire fence around the garden, she entered the house to shower once again to remove the lime and sulfur that smudged her hands and clothing. It was still a little early to go to brunch. Marlene liked to wait until mid-afternoon to go to the Midway Café to avoid the early crowd seeking to have breakfast early. Her phone alerted her noisily that she had a text message, and when she read the text, it was from Kimberly inviting her to the Corner Spot Café.

Previously Marlene had given Kimberly the same brush-off she'd given her coworker Bethany, promising to attend the next time. But that wouldn't be acceptable this time. She carefully replied, *Why don't you come by, and I'll make us breakfast?*

Kimberly countered the text. *I'm already here, waiting on you.* The Corner Spot Café was only three blocks from Marlene's home, so she quickly dressed and headed out the door. When she pulled up at the side of the restaurant, she could already see Kimberly, who was sitting at a table near the restaurant window. When Marlene exited her car, she was able to see the full table booth. She noticed Kimberly's brother Terry sitting at the table with her. Her smile quickly dissolved, and she displayed a look of anxiety. She walked into the restaurant and informed the greeter the person she was joining was already present. She advanced past several tables and booths before arriving at the table where Kimberly and Terry sat.

Kimberly quickly stood up to hug her friend. "I just took the initiative and decided to jump over to your neck of the woods to see you. I wasn't going to accept any more of your excuses after you cancelled the last couple of times."

Marlene was used to Kimberly's direct approach. "They weren't excuses. I get busy, but I do apologize for not making it up," Marlene said.

Terry stood up and extended his arms toward Marlene. "Don't I get a hug too? I haven't seen you in like ages. Wait, since you married that guy on the beach. I believe he is Stephanie's father, correct?" Marlene gave a halfhearted smile to Terry and did not return the embrace when he hugged her. She quickly sat down next to Kimberly.

"This guy showed up at my house wanting to do breakfast, and that was exactly what I was on my way to have with you. So, I just asked him to tag along so we can all get caught up," Kimberly explained. She could see the expression on Marlene's face that she'd come to know whenever Marlene wasn't comfortable with a situation. "Is it okay that I invited Terry? I didn't think it would be a problem."

Before Marlene could answer, Terry intervened. "What do you mean is it okay? We're like family. Hell, we are family. How is your daughter Stephanie anyway? I see her sometimes when I'm visiting my parents and she's over at your parents' house. She's really getting tall. She must get that from her father, because you're definitely average in height," Terry said and then laughed at his own joke. Marlene lifted the glass of ice water that was in front of her and continued drinking it until only ice was left in the glass. "Damn, someone is really thirsty this morning. You should have capped that one off with a big belch," he said.

Kimberly was mystified, knowing something was wrong. "Can you stop being goofy for five minutes?" Kimberly said to Terry, who had a confused look on his face. "Marlene, tell me what's wrong, and don't tell me there isn't anything wrong, because I know you." Terry was now attentive, refraining from being self-absorbed.

Not feeling pressured to answer Kimberly immediately, Marlene took a moment before replying. "Well, if you know me the way you say, why would you bring him here?" Marlene asked with boldness, no longer exhibiting the uncomfortable withdrawn behavior.

"Am I missing something here? Is there something going on between you guys I don't know about?" Kimberly asked.

"Why am I being discussed as though I am not sitting here? What have I done to you that would give you the gall to act like my mere presence is an insult to you?" Terry asked in animated fashion.

Marlene slapped the table with her hand and turned her chair directly facing Terry. The noise from slapping the table and the scraping of her chair across the floor drew the attention of all patrons. "Do you have selective amnesia? Or have you blocked out the day you raped me at your house, and impregnated me with a child. I was a virgin, you stole my innocence, and all this time you still act as though it never happened, while I've carried the burden of my father making me abort my child at the age of seventeen." Kimberly had a look of utter bewilderment on her face, but she could tell by Marlene's rare boldness with no regard for who heard her that there was truth in what she was saying.

"Do we have to talk about this so everyone can hear our business?" Terry mumbled.

"Yes, I've carried this secret all my life," Marlene said. "You think I give a damn about the fact these people can hear us and that you're uncomfortable?"

Terry thought for a moment, being ever so careful about his choice of words while Marlene continued to stare him down, waiting for his response.

"I'm sorry, I didn't know you were pregnant."

Kimberly was beyond stunned, but could no longer remain silent. "Terry, do you want to tell me what the hell you've done to my friend?"

"I didn't know about any pregnancy, and there was absolutely no rape. She consented to what we did. If I'd raped her, would we just be talking about this twenty years later?" Terry said, trying to justify his actions.

"Kimberly, I'm sorry I never told you what happened. I was young and so ashamed. I felt I compromised our friendship as a young girl by allowing Terry to take advantage of me. As a woman I know that I wasn't able to consent to sex as a minor and he was an adult, well over eighteen. In the State of Illinois that is called statutory rape," Marlene pronounced loudly, once again while facing her culprit."

Brenda the greeter walked over to the table and stated, "Excuse me, we do have other customers. If you and your party cannot keep your discussion to the confines of your table, I'm sorry, but I would have to ask you to leave."

Marlene smiled and responded, "I totally understand. If this man right here, whose mere presence is causing me anxiety, will not leave, I will leave, and I greatly apologize for the spectacle."

Kimberly without hesitation stated, "Terry, you need to leave."

Terry looked at Kimberly with disappointment, but he had no defense or recourse. He rose from his seat and exited the restaurant.

The greeter and one of the waitresses who accompanied her walked away from the table following Terry's departure. Kimberly reached across the table and grabbed Marlene's hand. "I didn't know." Marlene began to cry, and Kimberly rose from her seat to embrace her. "I'm here. I see you've been carrying a lot. Now that you have unburdened yourself of this, it's time to work on your healing." Hearing those encouraging words and the solace of being in Kimberly's arms, in spite of the fact that her violator was Kimberly's brother, meant the world to Marlene, and she continued to cry while basking in Kimberly's embrace. When she was able to gather herself, they exited the restaurant.

"Well, I guess you're stuck with me for the day. Terry drove me here," Kimberly said to bring humor to the situation.

"If you would've just come to the house for breakfast as I suggested, we would've already eaten by now, and my eyeliner wouldn't be a mess," Marlene said jokingly. "Honestly, I'm glad things turned out this way. I feel as though a weight has been lifted from me." They went back to Marlene's home, and she did make breakfast. After breakfast they talked for many hours. Marlene told Kimberly the entire story, starting from the day she came over to Kimberly's home to visit her and Terry invited her in even though his sister wasn't home. Marlene felt she owed it to Kimberly to finally tell her the entire story she had kept a secret for many years.

Kimberly now understood why at times Marlene could be antisocial. She asked Marlene if she wanted to press charges against Terry. Even though Terry was her brother, and the crime was committed a little more than two decades ago,

She realized Marlene was a minor at the time and her brother was a legal adult who took advantage of her. Terry was well aware that Marlene had a childhood crush on him, and this infuriated Kimberly even more.

Marlene was adamant that her goal wasn't to disrupt Terry's life. The fact was that seeing Terry today had aroused feelings she'd been running and hiding from for years. "When I saw Terry, it made me feel anxious and helpless in the same way I felt the day he had his way with me. Again, I say, I'm glad today happened. I needed to face him and the trauma I've avoided all this time. This was well overdue. Kimberly spent the entire day with Marlene, and she asked her to stay the night with her, especially since Stephanie was gone for the weekend. Later in the evening, while they were in the middle of watching a movie. Marlene's phone rang, and she paused the movie after seeing it was her mom who was calling.

"I know you told me how you feel, but I wanted to give you one last opportunity to be here concerning your father. They're saying if the antibiotics don't clear up his infection from the fall, it's a great possibility he may not make it through the night." It turned out her father had been bitten by a poisonous spider, which was the cause of the fever and fall he took. Marlene could hear the fear and desperation in her mother's voice, so she simply stated, "I'm on my way, Mom." Kimberly accompanied Marlene, and they were at MacNeal Hospital within ten minutes. When they entered the family waiting area, Marlene's two brothers and their families were present, and they all rushed to embrace and communicate with her. Honestly, Marlene was still not bent out of shape about the condition of her father.

She just didn't want him to make his transition without being present to show support for her family, whom she deeply cared about. After hugging her brothers, sister-in-laws, nieces, and nephews. Marlene could see her daughter Stephanie was sitting next to her grandmother. "Hey baby, how did you get here?" Marlene asked.

"Grandma called me about Granddad, and my father brought me." Just as Stephanie explained things to her mother, Daren came walking from around the corner after using the restroom.

"Hello, Marlene," Daren greeted.

"I don't think he should be here. Look, I know he's your father and I've never gotten in the way of you guys' relationship. But he and I cannot share the same space."

"It's not about him right now, it's about your father," Marlene's mother stated.

"Mom, I know you guys don't get along, but this is about Granddad. I needed to be here, and Dad brought me. It's not like I invited him to the house. This is a family emergency," Stephanie pleaded.

"I completely understand that, but he could wait downstairs or in another waiting area. He is no longer part of this family, and after what he did to me, I can't stand the sight of him," Marlene continued.

"I see she's still immature and can't let go of old history. I'll just go down to the other end where I saw another waiting area on my way from the bathroom," Daren said.

Marlene turned to Daren and pronounced, "Immature, you have the audacity to call me immature in front of my family as though you're in a position to pass judgment on me. Was I immature to divorce you after you had sex with our seventeen-year-old babysitter while our daughter was lying in her crib sleeping?" Daren didn't respond. Marlene had never told Stephanie the absolute truth about why her father and mother divorced. She only stated that they didn't get along well and that they made each other miserable. At the same time, Daren painted a different picture for Stephanie, which indicated that Marlene was bitter for no reason and fell out of love with him.

"Is that what happened, Dad? Is that really why you and Mom divorced?" Stephanie asked while facing her father.

"I don't think this is the right time to talk about this," Daren said. "I didn't come here for this. Honey, I came here to support you, not to be on trial about fictional events that happened a lifetime ago."

"You're right, Dad, this isn't the time for this, but I'm not asking you to divulge every detail. A simple yes or no would do on whether there's any truth to what Mom said about the babysitter."

All eyes were on Daren while Stephanie waited for an answer from her father. "If the events of our life together are just history, why can't you tell our daughter the truth, Daren?" Marlene stated. "You know what, I'm tired of being the heavy. Stephanie, your stepmother Madeline used to be the babysitter we're talking about. Soon after I divorced him, months later when she turned eighteen, he married her. I used to be embarrassed that my husband chose a teenage girl over me. But today is a new day. I only take responsibility for mistakes I made in my own life." Kimberly touched Marlene's shoulder to let her know her support was there.

"You're lonely and bitter. You try to destroy other people's lives so that they can be miserable just like you," Daren attacked.

Marlene's brother Travis quickly interrupted. "Hold on right there, sir. You watch how you speak to my sister. Up until now you've received a pass because I'm just learning what happened along with my niece and the rest of the family. My father is sick, and I won't disrespect him or my mother by wasting time on you in this moment. I suggest you leave before I do something I'll regret," Travis stated with authority.

"This is a public hospital. If my daughter wants me to be here, I will be here. I will move to the other end, but you don't have the authority to tell me to leave this hospital."

"I think you should leave, Dad," Stephanie said very calmly. Daren stood and looked at Stephanie for a moment in disbelief as she asked him to leave.

"Oh, and just so we're clear," Marlene said. "My truth today wasn't because I'm bitter, it's actually because I'm better. And Daren, I forgive you for what you did to me. I will no longer carry around the heavy baggage of unforgiveness. You can pick your own bags up and carry them with you on your way out." Daren stared at Marlene momentarily, then walked out of the recovery department with no further response.

"Why haven't you ever told anyone about this?" Travis asked his sister. Marlene hunched her shoulders and gave Travis a halfhearted smile. He walked over to his sister and hugged her, feeling there wasn't anything else left to be said. Marlene cried in her brother's arms. Once again, her direct transparency was much-needed therapy, unburdening herself from the past, which had held her hostage for so many years.

"Mom, I know you hate confrontation, but I'm learning I have to face my issues and fears. Not run from them, or ignore them. I love you to pieces, but I admit I partially blamed you for not protecting me from Dad when he made me have an abortion when that's not what I wanted."

Alice lowered her head and then softly stated, "I truly understand better now, and I'm sorry I didn't have the courage to stand up to your father. But I don't think this is the time to discuss this while your father is in the woods until morning." Stephanie looked on to see what her mother's response would be.

"You're right, Mom. I just want you to know that today is amnesty forgiveness day for me. So, I do forgive Dad, and anyone else that has wronged me in any way. I take full responsibility for my life and the way I've handled my issues. My own unwillingness to deal with my issues and my unwillingness to forgive have affected relationships. I've been socially awkward and I've developed a lack of trust, mostly with men. Today though, I can honestly say, my issues are no longer unresolved."

THE ISSUE OF VAL!DAT!ON

CHAPTER 7

IT WAS COOLER THAN normal for a late spring day as Norma pulled her head from under her blankets trying to pinpoint the repeated tapping sound that had awakened her. Her bedroom was unusually dark, her curtains were blowing inward, and now she was able to identify the noise that woke her. It was the rain hitting the awning outside of her bedroom window. She looked at her flashing radio clock that continuously blinked twelve a.m. She then looked over at her DVR player, which was also flashing, giving her indication the power had gone out in her condominium at some point last night. She quickly grabbed her phone from the nightstand while flipping her blanket and twirling her legs to the floor all in one motion. It was three minutes after six, and Norma customarily woke up at five-twenty. She worked for a downtown Social Security office as supervisor administrator, but her morning commute was twenty-five to thirty minutes from her condominium.

Moreover, Norma woke up early daily, because she had routines that had to be carried out prior to going to work, and she didn't like to rush. "Damn it," Norma yelled out as she grabbed a pair of underwear off the back of the chair that sat before her vanity mirror on the way to her bathroom to shower. Norma enjoyed making her own coffee before work, and ordinarily she would have a cup while putting on her makeup. Prior to leaving her condo, she would fill her coffee mug with more coffee to transport to the office. Norma routinely would put a bagel in her toaster oven to eat before leaving the house. Most times she would only eat half of the bagel with strawberry cream cheese. She would give the other half of her bagel to her neighbor's cat, Melony, that climbed over to her balcony in search of her treat every morning. Melony enjoyed the strawberry cream cheese more so than the bagel itself.

Norma exited her shower, patting her body with a bath towel on the way to her kitchen to start her coffeemaker. She never wiped her body with the towel. She needed her pores to be susceptible to her morning add-ons. When she looked into the refrigerator to pull out her French vanilla coffee creamer and the cream cheese for her bagel, it dawned on her that she'd forgotten to go to the grocery store yesterday to purchase her French vanilla creamer after her workout. The amount she had left in the container was not enough for her desired taste. "This is not going to be my day," Norma pronounced, then looked out of her kitchen window to check if it was still raining now that she no longer heard the rain beating down against her awning and windows in the condominium.

The rain had let up some, but it was still drizzling, as she could see raindrops falling in puddles on the community patio. She rushed back into the room to spray a mist of perfume in the air, and she walked through the falling mist of the perfume. Norma carried out this routine twice before leaving. She was finicky about spraying anything directly on her skin. After rubbing baking soda under her arms, she sat down at her vanity mirror affixed to her dresser, which was filled with makeup, assorted nail polishes, and her treasured perfume collection. She started putting her foundation on and followed with putting on her eyeliner. Norma became frustrated, wiped her face and started over, because the line wasn't flawlessly drawn under her eyes. She picked up her smartphone and could see that it was six-twenty-seven. Norma rarely made mistakes with her makeup, and she knew her error was due to the fact she was rushing.

She made a call to the Social Security office to inform them she would be an hour late, and she also gave instructions to employees whom she managed. After Norma made the call, she returned to her kitchen to make her bagel. She could hear her neighbor's cat Melony crying and scratching at her patio door. After she'd placed the bagel in the saucer on the patio for Melony to eat, she took a bite of her own bagel and walked calmly back to her beautification station. Norma would much rather be late for work than arrive with her appearance less than the standard she'd set for herself.

She finished her makeup and smiled back at herself in the mirror, satisfied with her artistic accomplishment. She then stepped into her orange backless ChicNora fitted dress with the V-neck designed to frame up the cleavage of her voluptuous breasts. Norma, ever the professional, retrieved her black, one-button blazer that complemented her well-put-together frame. Norma was forty-two years of age, regularly ate balanced meals, and frequented the gym one hour a day four days a week. Norma had never had any children, marrying at twenty-five, but getting divorced after three years at age twenty-eight. Inevitably, since her divorce, Norma dated occasionally. However, she didn't spend her energy trying to build romantic relationships at this point. Norma exited her condo and walked over to her assigned parking space to slide into her 2020 Lexus ES 350.

She glanced at her phone to get a grasp of the time, because she wanted to stop off at the Sonic car wash that she was a valued member at before heading in to work. She wouldn't have time to have the inside detailed, but she did have time to dash into the drive-through to get a wash and wax so her car would display the gloss she was most comfortable with. Everything had to be in order for Norma. She felt anything associated with her was a representation of her. This kind of mindset was birthed from the foundation of her upbringing at the hands of her parents. Norma was an adorable child, and in addition to how pretty she was, Norma had rosy, chubby cheeks, and wherever she went, she received a lot of attention from people either complimenting her chubby cheeks or trying to pinch them.

As Norma got older, her parents, Stephen and Jacqueline, drilled her about having an immaculate appearance. They conditioned her to believe that one day, regardless of her own achievements, she would meet a man with wealth, and he would take care of her. As a kid, Norma didn't enjoy wearing dresses and stockings to school while other girls wore jeans and tennis shoes. She was sent to a private institution for high school that required her to wear uniforms. Her parents obsessively imposed upon her to always have noticeable ironed creases in her clothes, and if her shoes weren't new, they had to be cleaned to perfection. Norma was a very pretty girl, with the kind of beauty that forced people to stare rather than glance. As she moved into adulthood, she was considered a good catch, and she realized the power she had over men. She no longer required convincing and tutoring from her parents. She bought into what her parents had been selling her since she was a child. During her final semester in college, she met Ronald, and after a few years of dating they married.

Norma couldn't understand why her husband was so casual about his appearance, and she religiously questioned his career ambitions. Ronald had a business degree from Harvard, but he worked as a social worker. This frustrated Norma to no end. She couldn't fathom why Ronald was so involved with a community he couldn't relate to, nor was he from. Ronald's family owned a chain of upscale restaurants across the city of Chicago, and his family had just opened a new restaurant in Oak Park, a suburb west of Chicago. Ronald's father wanted him to market the new restaurant and oversee the accounting of all their restaurants, rather than paying non-family members for these services. However, Ronald wasn't interested. He made it clear to his parents and Norma several times that his passion was for helping people.

Ronald did have a trust fund that he was legally entitled to at age twenty-five, but it was laden with conditions of marriage and career goals. Ronald set out to make it on his own without accepting the advantage most people weren't privy to. He appreciated his parents and was proud of their accomplishments, but he wanted to make his mark on the world by giving and serving others. As Norma started to advance in her own career, she began networking, rubbing elbows with upper-echelon corporates whom she felt could open doors for her that her education could not. Whenever there were events, she would chide Ronald for his casual dress and talk over him whenever her colleagues would ask what it was he did for a living. Distance ensued, and the two grew further and further apart. After three years and no use of the trust fund, Norma asked Ronald for a divorce. He eventually submitted to Norma's request, because he'd become turned off and was frankly appalled by her self-serving drive. To this day, Norma continued a relationship with Ronald's parents, but she remained bitter toward Ronald. She literally had disdain for him for not taking advantage of the privileges she desperately wanted access to.

Norma went through the car wash, and she turned up the volume to the motivational speaker Wayne Dyer, whom she listened to while driving.

Strangely enough, the scents from the soap the car wash used were intoxicating to Norma. She often came to the car wash even when her car was not in need of cleaning.

As she entered the office building where she worked, she spoke to other managers and executives. Still and all, she looked right past the building's security personnel and members of the housekeeping department. Norma would only communicate with these employees if she had need for them. She had been told in college by one of her sorority sisters that interacting with people considered beneath her would damage her image, and reduce her to their level of mediocrity. Norma bought into this mindset and still functioned in this manner. She exited the elevator on the eleventh floor, which was the entire Social Security department. She saw one of the building's engineers coming down the hall, and she stood by the door and waited for him to open the door for her. The engineer did oblige Norma by opening the glass door, but he marveled that Norma walked through the door without acknowledging him or thanking him.

"If you're not on the phone, then you're not working. I will get a log report of the length of time you people are at your stations without servicing customers," Norma yelled to no one in particular as she walked into her office.

"The nerve of her to arrive late, come in here barking out orders, and doesn't speak to anyone. If either one of us would enter the workplace over an hour late for duty, there would certainly be some disciplinary action," Moorene, one of the Tele-Service Representatives, said to Charlotte as she walked back into her cubicle coming from getting coffee.

"That's true, but you're not the boss, so to avoid the disciplinary action get on the phone and earn your pay," Charlotte said jokingly.

"You're such a company person. Social Security or Norma are not paying you to speak on their behalf," Moorene shot back. Charlotte and Moorene were more than coworkers. Charlotte had referred Moorene for the job, and she was hired based on Charlotte's recommendation. Moreover, Moorene also was in a long-term relationship with Charlotte's cousin Marcus.

Norma walked into her office, but before sitting down at her desk, she wiped off the fingerprints she noticed on her Director of the Year award that was positioned behind her desk on the wall. As soon as she sat down in her chair, her secretary, Diane, walked briskly into her office shuffling sticky notes she'd written phone numbers with messages on.

"I'm glad you're here," Diane said. "Mr. Soto has called twice for you, and he wants you to call him as soon as you get in. Oh, and I hope you remember that corporate is sending someone here this morning to monitor how this office is running."

Diane was about to continue when Norma abruptly interjected: "Did you just walk into my office without knocking, without giving me a chance to sit down properly or take a sip of my coffee?"

Diane set the messages on Norma's desk and slightly rolled her eyes. "I'm sorry, I thought you may have wanted to be informed of the things that took place prior to you arriving for work. I'll be at my desk," Diane said as she turned to walk out of Norma's office.

"Diane," Norma called out to her secretary, stopping her in her tracks, but Diane did not turn around to face Norma.

"Yes," she answered.

"Call Mr. Soto and tell him I will send him a report on the recommendations of the consultant coming to monitor our office after the evaluation is complete. In addition, please get me an assignment sheet and the call logs from yesterday."

Still facing the outside of the door, Diane answered, "I'll be back shortly with your request."

"Oh, and Diane," Norma called out once again.

"Yes, Ms. Powell?"

"Get in the habit of facing me when I communicate with you. When discussing business, that position can be considered rude and definitely unprofessional. Over and above that, those shoes you have on doesn't match your outfit. You're my assistant, and I implore you to represent me well. Especially when we're having guests, appearance is everything."

Diane was not pleased with Norma's critique of her outfit, but unfortunately, she was used to this form of judgment from her superior. Within a couple of minutes, Diane knocked and re-entered Norma's office with the call logs from the previous two days. She set them down in front of Norma on her desk and stated, "I'll be back shortly with the assignment sheet you requested as soon as I make copies of it."

Norma picked up the stack of papers and began looking at the call log while strategically looping her finger on her other hand to unbutton her blazer. She scanned the first sheet thoroughly and quickly flipped over to the second page. She ran her finger down multiple column sections to help keep her eyes affixed on the desired location. She quickly rose from her seat and walked out of her office, past her secretary's desk and into the call center, which was sectioned off by cubicles. "I am in no mood for apathy today. If you are caught creating downtime while on the clock when you should be servicing clients the government is paying you to serve, I assure you, heads will roll today," Norma calmly conveyed her threat.

"Is that the way you lead your team, with an iron fist?" Norma turned around to see the corporate hired consultant Daphne Atwood standing next to her secretary Diane.

Shocked by Daphne's presence, and obviously exposed by her behavior, all Norma could do was extend her hand to say, "Hi, I'm Norma, and I'm the branch director for the Southeast location."

Daphne didn't extend her hand right away, choosing to gaze at Norma up and down with her eyes before finally giving voice too.

"I know exactly who you are. Do you know who I am?" Daphne asked with mystery.

"No, ma'am. I'm aware we were expecting someone from corporate today, so I must assume you're the representative that came to monitor how this office operates."

At that time Daphne extended her hand to shake Norma's. "You're partially correct. My name is Daphne Atwood, and although I was commissioned by corporate to conduct a service at this location, I do not work for the government. I conduct evaluations for many organizations across our great states. Please let that be the last assumption you make about me during my tenure here. Norma, what's your last name?"

"My last name is Powell. Please, let's go inside my office so we may talk further and I can provide you with whatever you need," Norma said while motioning in the direction of her office and starting to maneuver in that direction.

"Ms. Powell, I can't see how this office operates from inside your comfortable office. Make no mistake, I will review documents at my request, I will monitor whether you're following government protocol, and I will be interacting with your staff as well. I'll be monitoring day-to-day operations, and overall performance is what I am here to monitor. During my findings I will submit a corrective action plan to you and the organization. Lastly, I've asked you not to make further assumptions about me while I'm here. You called me Daphne. I prefer we keep it professional and you address me as Mrs. Atwood, and I will address you as Ms. Powell.

"Yes, Mrs. Atwood," Norma responded. Diane walked away, heading back to her desk after hearing the phone ring. She was very much enjoying seeing Norma in this vulnerable and submissive position she so often put others in. At the end of staff's phone calls, they could be seen looking outside of their cubicles to witness who was speaking to Norma in this manner.

"Ms. Powell, those are government recipients your staff are speaking to on the phone, correct?" Daphne asked in a calm tone.

"Yes, that is whom they are supposed to be speaking with anyway," Norma carefully responded.

"Then can you please explain to me why you think it was appropriate to yell and threaten your staff while they are servicing clients on the phone? Is this how you instill morale with employees?"

Norma paused and took a deep breath. She could see she had already gotten off on the wrong foot with Daphne, and she could also see that Daphne wasn't going to make it easy for her to redeem herself. "I apologize for my level of frustration, but I reassure you this is not the normal practice that I communicate with my employees," Norma explained.

"Ms. Powell, I believe these are government employees and as for whether or not that display is normal practice, that remains to be seen. Now, I'd very much like to see your assignment sheet for today. I want to engage with the staff you manage, when they're on breaks or lunches. I can also have dialogue with them in between calls with clients. If they're unwilling to speak with me on their time, please allow them grace to get back to their work stations considering they may exceed scheduled time."

Norma was apprehensive about how to respond. "I was a little tardy this morning. I have yet to fill out the assignment sheet, but it's still way early into the shift. Our lunches have not yet begun. We don't list breaks on the assignment sheet, because the team would rather have an hour lunch, rather than a thirty-minute lunch and two fifteen-minute breaks."

Daphne smiled before responding. "To my understanding fifteen-minute breaks after two hours are in the collective bargaining agreement between your organization and the union. To start a practice outside of what has been already agreed upon is definitely liable to a grievance."

Norma offered no response initially, but finally stated, "Mrs. Atwood, it would be a violation only if one of the employees felt they were being violated. However, this is something that was brought to my attention by the staff, and we both agreed this could work to the benefit of both sides. I have been over this office for four years to date. There have yet to be any discrepancies or grievances concerning this matter."

Daphne was not at all offended by Norma's protocol rationale. She was actually impressed by Norma's ability to communicate thoroughly what had worked well for the office. This was ultimately the purpose she had been sent there.

"I stand corrected. Let's say we go to your office and get started on that assignment sheet. Your staff should have things outlined for them so they have clear expectations."

Norma was surprised Daphne was receptive to her feedback. To this point she felt her authority and competency had been questioned from the moment Daphne entered the workspace. Daphne followed Norma into her office and took a seat. Norma was about to call Diane to bring her the assignment sheet she had requested prior to Daphne's arrival, but it was already on her desk. Daphne sat in front of Norma's desk surveying the contents in the office, mostly the plaques and awards on the wall, but she remained on task.

"Which one of your staff has been identified as your floor lead and/or preceptor for new employees?" Daphne asked.

Norma began quickly filling out the assignment sheet while still answering Daphne. "There isn't a floor lead as you call it, and I train anyone coming in as a new employee. Again, I've been over this office for four years, and I have yet to miss a day of work."

Daphne quickly retorted, "That's absurd. What if you need to be off for an extended period of time? Accidents and illnesses are beyond our control at times. Are you saying this entire government office is totally dependent on your presence and good health?"

Norma absorbed the context of the way Daphne labeled the stability of the office, and it made her realize the unintentional liabilities she was placing on the Social Security office. "Mrs. Atwood, would you like a cup of coffee? I'll be done with the assignment sheet in about two minutes," Norma asked once she looked up and noticed Daphne staring directly over at the assignment sheet she was filling out.

"No, I'm fine, but I'd very much appreciate it if you would answer my question about identifying an employee to be a lead. Select an employee who has your vision, and who understands the purpose of this office. You should have identified that person within six months of your arrival to this office."

"Mrs. Atwood, Bridget is a long-time employee well beyond my arrival to this office. She is that person for me, but she is not the lead, and she has no desire to be one. She has been working at this location the entire fourteen years that it has been in existence. All the other employees respect her and come to her for direction when they don't know the answer to an issue that arises. I am confident in her abilities and trust things will run smoothly in my absence. I do understand your point about extended time off beyond my control. In a case like that, corporate would have to send someone to this office to manage until I return. I will, however, identify someone, because as stated, Bridget has no desire to be in management."

"You have a lot of confidence in an employee who has been in the same position with absolutely no desire for advancement. I'd be leery of an individual that's content and afraid of progression."

Norma heard Daphne's critique but opted not to place stock in it. "Here is the completed assignment sheet. I'm ready to go back onto the floor to assist you in whatever you need."

It didn't go unnoticed by Daphne the clever way Norma discounted her opinion about choosing a floor lead using her protocol. Once again Daphne did not take offense. She was merely offering a suggestion in the best interests of the organization. "You've neglected to list the Tele-Service Representative that will be relieving staff for their lunches. The assignment sheet also doesn't reflect whom you've assigned the responsibility of bypassing the phone lines to the automated system when the office closes for operation."

Norma quickly answered, "I didn't assign anyone because I relieve the people for their lunches. I reroute calls outside of service operation to the automated line system as well."

Daphne could tell Norma was getting somewhat peeved by her analysis and input. Nevertheless, she took note of how Norma was able to absorb it without being confrontational or unprofessional. "Ms. Powell, based on what you've communicated, it's clear that you have a difficult time with relinquishing control to others."

Norma couldn't hide her displeasure at Daphne's inequitable assessment of her. "Excuse me, Mrs. Atwood, I don't exactly understand what's your issue with me, but you can focus on monitoring and reporting on how my office runs. You are here as a consultant to the government, but that doesn't give you license to personally appraise my life."

Daphne sat down in one of the two chairs sitting in front of Norma's desk. "That's exactly what I am doing. My assessment is strictly pertaining to the job. I feel you're not utilizing the organization's protocol and/or the resources that are available to you. In addition, I honestly feel you're putting this office in jeopardy. "Can I speak off the record for a moment and be frank with you?"

Norma placed her pen on the desk and sat back in her executive office chair and stated, “You can be Frank, Martha, David or whomever you feel the need to be, just come correct in your approach.”

Daphne required more assurance before proceeding, “This will be off the record correct?”

Norma quickly answered, “Yes, please say what it is you need to say.”

Daphne set her purse on the floor next to the chair she was sitting in. “I compute that everything has to be carried out in impeccable fashion with you. It has to be done by you and facilitated by you. Sometimes we may have a comfortable way of doing things, never realizing there could be a better, more efficient way of going about things. Ways that could be beneficial to us, the people around us, and the organization altogether. In this case we’re dealing with a process, so this cannot be totally about a single individual. Do you understand what I’m trying to say to you?” Daphne sought out confirmation.

“You haven’t said anything for me to understand,” Norma replied. “You asked that this be off the record, then you made some indirect statements, but I’m trying to figure out how any of what you said applies to me.”

Daphne felt Norma was now speaking to her in a condescending manner. “I don’t know why I bother with some of you people. Well, here it is without the sugar or the coat. I see you with the impeccable makeup, the name-brand clothes and shoes. You don’t trust anyone to do anything for you, because you’re some sort of control freak who masks her issues by making sure things get done your way. I gather you were some pretty little girl who was always told you were beautiful. Did you marry some privileged prince charming who needed a showpiece on his arm to validate him in the same way you desire to be validated?" Norma continued to listen, and although she was appalled, she did not interrupt. "If I have you pegged correctly, you were probably tardy this morning because the outfit you wanted to wear wasn't available, or you couldn't leave the house until your makeup was flawless. Ms. Powell, if that's how you choose to conduct your life, that is clearly your prerogative. But you cannot, will not, impose your issues to be validated on this office."

Norma waited patiently for Daphne to complete her personal commentary. She was all set to blast Daphne until the last statement about the reason she was late this morning. "What would make you come to those conclusions about me? You've only met me less than an hour ago," Norma asked defensively, but clearly she was seeking to find out how Daphne could be so clear-cut in her assessment.

Daphne sat upright in her chair with her back perfectly arched while reaching down to pick up her handbag off the floor. "Ms. Powell, I don't think conclusions have any relevancy in this set of circumstances. The question isn't whether these are my conclusions about you, it's more about whether they are specific to you, and whether this office is functioning in accordance with governmental policies."

"Mrs. Atwood, what have I given off in the past few moments that has led to this insight on your part to sum me up in this way? I'm really curious to know that."

Daphne smiled and adjusted her blouse so it was no longer hinged to her brassiere. "The fact that you're asking me that question gives complete indication you have this insatiable need to be validated by others. Okay, let's say my estimate of you is off kilter. Why then do you need for me to reiterate and explain what I was very distinct in communication about? Now can we get back to this assignment sheet, and my overall objective for being here today?"

Instinctively, Norma wanted to be defensive. This was a mechanism that had always worked for her, and if it did not work, it simply bought her time to come up with something to ward off people who identified more about her than just her appearance.

"Mrs. Atwood, you asked me if you could step outside of business for a moment to speak off the record. I believe you referred to it as being frank. But now that I've sought out clarity, you want to ascend back to the seat of professionalism. It appears you have a willingness to control the narrative as well. If you can dish out this kind of critiquing, surely you should be able to withstand it."

Daphne wanted to move on, so she superficially caved in to Norma's attempt to save face. "Fine, you are right, and I stand corrected. Be that as it may, on this assignment sheet I see two areas that you have not listed anyone for follow-up calls, and I still think you should list the staff breaks because it's protocol without future backlash."

Norma quickly shot back, "And as I've already explained to you, we have a method here that compiles the breaks with the lunches. As for the follow-up calls, I didn't designate anyone because I facilitate those calls."

"Once again, Ms. Powell, you are putting this office at risk by limiting your staff to minimal knowledge of how this office should be run. Everything cannot be totally dependent upon you to get done. Things happen, and we must prepare for them, Ms. Powell."

Norma quickly retorted, "Understood. I'll work on that. It's obvious I have so much to work on even though my office has run with precision for the past four years prior to your arrival."

Daphne set the assignment sheet back on Norma's desk and stood to pronounce, "Your lack of cooperation is something I don't have time for. I will submit my report on my findings about this office."

Norma stood. "Oh, leaving so soon? I thought you would be around for at least a couple of days, Daphne," she said to get a rise out of Mrs. Atwood.

"When I submit my branch report, it will include the way I observed you yelling at employees in a hostile tone."

Norma projected a show of confidence by staying even keel, showing no signs of concern. "If that pleases you to do so, because I stood up to you, then by all means go right ahead. Please include in your report how you became personal with me, and clinically diagnosed my thought process. Oh, for your information, I recorded the entire conversation on my phone."

Daphne was flabbergasted by Norma's quick retaliation, but she was not angry with Norma. She smiled and nodded her head in Norma's direction to validate the stalemate with a non-verbal cue. Daphne then turned to exit Norma's office.

Norma sat back in her chair, feeling accomplished that she had managed to subdue Daphne's intimidating tactics. Even still, she couldn't deny many of the things Daphne said while critiquing her were quite true.

Diane came to the door, knocked and waited to be acknowledged before entering. "Is she leaving already? I hope we did well. She didn't look too pleased when she passed by my desk on the way to the elevator."

Norma responded with confidence, "I think we did rather well. I don't think we'll be getting any backlash from the head office in Washington, D.C."

"You have a phone call on line three from your ex-husband Ronald. He called earlier but I told him you were busy with a client. Shall I reiterate to him that you are tied up, or would you like to take his call?"

Norma, was inquisitive as to why Ronald was calling her, but she felt compelled to speak with him. "I'll take his call. Please close the door on your way out. Oh, and Diane. Thank you. I apologize for snapping at you earlier about walking into my office unannounced. You've always done that, and I shouldn't change an ongoing practice midstream, without giving you indications of the new expectation. So, let's establish this going forward. If my door is open, you may enter as you always have. However, if my door is closed, I need you to knock. Obviously there must be a pertinent reason the door is closed in the first place. Are we in agreement on that?"

Diane was shocked by Norma's apology. She had never apologized to her for anything in four years. Diane most certainly had never witnessed this form of humility from Norma. "I accept your apology. I will knock if the door is closed, and thank you for revisiting this with me. I'll get out of your way so you can take your phone call," Diane said before exiting the office and closing the door behind her.

Norma pushed the button for line three, and answered very graciously. "Good morning to you, Ronald, how are you today?"

Very surprised by Norma's courtesy and willingness to oblige his phone call, Ronald returned the pleasantry. "I'm doing well actually, thank you for asking. How are you today?"

Norma let out a small sigh and stated, "I guess I'm doing pretty good. I can't complain."

"Wonderful," Ronald responded. "Well, I've called the house a couple of times and I've left voice messages with no response. That's the only reason I'm calling you at your place of work. I was completing the necessary paperwork of the will I'm putting in place, and I realized that we're still one another's beneficiaries on the insurance policy. We need to change it and each select someone else to be the beneficiary."

"Why do we need to do that? I'm okay with you being the beneficiary, especially when you're paying the premiums. The only people I'm concerned about if something were to happen to me is the wellbeing of my mother and goddaughter. Honestly, I trust that you would do the right thing. Moreover, I already have an additional insurance policy that covers me." There was an awkward silence momentarily after Norma spoke. "Ronald, are you still there?" Norma inquired.

"Yes, I'm still here. I guess I'm surprised this call is going a lot better than I expected. I'm surprised you're able to be this cordial with me."

Norma decided to take this opportunity to address her past behavior. "Ronald, I want to apologize to you for behaving selfishly and immaturely during our marriage, and even after our marriage. You are a remarkable man. I admire the fact that you have character. You have a heart for others when you very well could've been privileged by your parents' wealth. I've always regretted our divorce, but today I'm able to acknowledge that I am the reason for the divorce. Maybe I'm foolish for trying to acknowledge my behavior after the fact, but I am truly sorry, Ronald."

Ronald quickly responded, "Wow, well first off, I don't think it's foolish at all. I think it takes character and maturity to be able to look at one-self and accept the fact there's room for growth. We all have room for growth. Anyhow, I accept your apology, and this may sound crazy, but I still love you, Norma, and I think we owe it to ourselves to try again. I don't want to have any regrets."

"Are you sure that's what you want?" Norma asked, in awe of Ronald's plea.

"Yes, I'm sure. I think a better question is, is this something you want?"

Without hesitation Norma responded, "I can't think of anything I want more right now." Norma was containing herself while on the phone, but she was leaping inside to even be treading the waters of reconnection with Ronald.

"I have to go down to Springfield today to get a client of mine set up with her new residence. I won't make it back until late tonight sometime, but can we have dinner tomorrow night?" Ronald asked.

Norma continued to project that she was calm and contained. "Yes, I think tomorrow night will be good for me. What time are we meeting, and where are we going?"

Ronald thought for a second and then responded, "Let's meet at eight o'clock, and if it's okay with you, I would like to make dinner for you at our home."

Norma was shocked that Ronald referred to his home as their home. Norma had lived there for three years but wanted no part of the house in the divorce. "I'll see you tomorrow night then, Mr. Powell."

Norma hung up the phone, basking in a state of euphoria after having this unexpected interaction with her ex-husband. Diane knocked on the office door and was granted permission to enter. "Ms. Powell, I am going to lunch. I have forwarded the calls to your line until I get back. Would you like me to bring you anything? I'm going to Pompeii's on Taylor Street."

"No thank you, Diane, enjoy your lunch." Diane was headed out of the door but stepped back to say, "I heard how that lady spoke to you. She was really rude, but you handled it well, boss lady." Norma smiled and chuckled at Diane's statement. "I'm surprised to see you laughing, Ms. Powell. She wasn't the friendliest person I've come in contact with," Diane said.

Norma replied, "I'm smiling because Daphne is equivalent to something I heard my mother's pastor say quite frequently as a child, and today it has come full circle as to what he was trying to convey."

"What's that, Ms. Powell?"

Norma smiled, and stated, "Learn to eat the meat, and spit out the bone."

THE ISSUE OF RACISM

CHAPTER 8

IT WAS A BEAUTIFUL spring day, and the weather was very pleasant after coming off a brutal Chicago winter. There was plenty of sunshine, a nice warm breeze, and the current temperature was seventy-one degrees. Carl stepped out of his Black Nissan Pathfinder SUV along with his neighbor Milo after parking behind the back of the museum on the cusp of Lake Michigan. He looked around to see how far his friends and coworkers were behind. They trailed him after their pickup basketball game at the YMCA. Historically, after their games, they would park by the lake, drink some beers, and talk about sports and life in general. Manny and his cousin Paco were blasting their horn and yelling as they pulled into a space. Their arrival antics drew attention, along with strange looks from others who were already enjoying the sights out onto the lake with their company. After the light changed, three more cars pulled into the secluded area just off the lake behind where Carl parked his car. Manny was a coworker of Carl's at Murphy's Steel and Wood.

Paul, who worked as a firefighter, was one of Carl's childhood friends. He also had played high school and college basketball at Northwestern. Paul wasn't always able to attend every tournament game they had because of his rotating schedule at the fire department, but his teammates understood the reasoning for his inconsistencies. He opened his trunk so that his music would be able to be heard by everyone within a fifty-yard radius of where they parked. Paul was accompanied by his brother Maurice and one of his coworkers, Silva.

"I hope you brought enough beers this time, Paul. It was ten of us last time and you bought a case of Budweiser when you know we drink a whole hell of a lot more beers than that," Carl said as he walked over to Paul's truck to get a beer out of the cooler.

"I apologized to you guys once before. I told you I made a mistake. Besides, it was Silva's turn to buy, and he bought two cases of Coronas," Paul responded.

"I notice every time it's a guy's turn to buy the brews, the beer changes in relation to ethnicity," Steven stated with laughter.

"You have something against Coronas, bro? No one complained when you people brought that good ole boy Beck's beer the time before. No one I know drinks that piss. I tell you, every culture really has a different taste bud," Manny immediately chimed in. "That's a complete understatement if I ever heard one."

Everyone began to laugh, relating to what Manny was conveying. "So, when you say 'you people,' you really mean white people," Steven said.

"Yes, I mean white people. Black people and Latinos don't drink Beck's and Budweiser," Manny shot back.

"So, when it's Nick's and my turn to buy, because we're the white guys, we need to be conscious of buying Old English Eight-Hundred with some Modelos?" Steven said.

"Hey, watch that, Oxford boy, nobody here drinks no damn malt liquor," Julius said. He didn't like Steven or Nick, who were also Carl's coworkers.

The last two years when they'd played pickup games or been in basketball tournaments together, Julius made it clear he didn't want to be teammates with Nick and Steven.

"All right guys, calm down and have a beer. We're not about to get into racial stereotypes. I get enough of that watching the news listening to your president, with his biased depictions of other nationalities," Paul said as he began to toss everyone a beer who didn't have one.

"Hey, who sings that song, I like the bass line and I've heard that voice before?" Steven asked Paul, but before Paul could answer, Julius interjected, "That's an R&B artist by the name of Kem. He's what we call a crooner, and I'm sure his lyrics are out of your range. Don't hurt yourself trying to keep up."

Recognizing the tension, Tracy, who was a neighbor of Carl's, asked, "Where is Perry? I thought he was riding with you guys."

Maurice, who drove one of the vehicles, answered, "He was going to carpool with us to the water, but he got a phone call, and he was arguing with someone about picking up his kids from somewhere." Carl's interest was piqued because he had given Perry his wallet before their game, because he didn't have any pockets on his gym shorts to secure his wallet. Carl didn't want to put his wallet in the locker room of the YMCA due to items going missing in the past.

"He has my wallet. He should've told me he was leaving so I could retreive my property from him. That guy constantly has issues with the mother of his two children, it's literally every week it seems like." Tracy nodded his head, indicating he was in agreement with Carl.

"Baby mama drama is what they call it, right?" Steven said, and laughed along with Nick and Manny. Julius looked at Steven with a piercing look of contempt.

"Hey fellas, the next time we play that team that calls themselves The Triplets, with the six-foot-eight guy playing center, we have to have whoever's guarding him play out on the perimeter to pull him away from the basket. We need to be out there to keep the defense honest. Otherwise, he is going to camp in that lane, get easy buckets, and clog up the middle." Manny announced.

Silva quickly stated on the matter, "I agree. I told Nick I would switch off with him." Silva received some funny looks from guys on the team.

"No offense, but you just can't handle that guy in the paint. He was man-handling you in the post the first half," Maurice explained.

"I'm sorry, but that guy is as strong as an ox. It's like wrestling with a gorilla in the paint," Nick said.

Many of the guys laughed at Nick's submissive admission, but Julius was offended and immediately made it known. "What the hell, man, if one of you white boys makes another back-door racist comment, it's going to be a problem out here on this asphalt."

"White boys, so we're referring to one another by color now? I didn't mean anything intentional by it. I was just saying the guy was strong, and I was no match for him in the paint." Nick interjected.

Julius yelled back, "Well, say that then. Don't be making references to an ox or gorillas. You know damn well historically those were labels placed on black people by your forefathers."

"Come on, guys, let's settle down," Carl said. "It wasn't that deep. Nick, I know you didn't mean anything by it, but it can be perceived to be offensive to someone who doesn't know you. References about gorillas and African Americans at the same time are a touchy subject with my people."

Steven was about to respond, but Silva blurted out without hesitation, "Really, bro, I hear where you're coming from, but if you're going to be politically correct and police appropriate vernacular on race, hold the same standard when guys are making ethnic comments in regards to beer, or Oxford when referring to white people."

"Wow, Silva, I can't believe you went there, bro. I was only trying to make sure things wouldn't get out of hand. I thought we came here to throw back a few brews and talk about the game and the upcoming tournament," Carl said.

"Well, yeah, but Nick has a point, and so does Silva. I wish you would police some of that racially insensitive garbage that comes out of the mouths of people who share the same culture as you," Steven added.

"Are you referring to me? I don't like your white ass anyway. The only reason I haven't put you down is because of Carl and the fact that he works with you guys. But make no mistake, you make one more animal comparison or baby mama reference, my love and respect for Carl won't save you from these paws," Julius said with fury. Paul walked down the pathway in between Julius and Steven, sensing the escalation of the matter.

"Jules, calm down, man. This really isn't that deep, and we can talk about this without any threats of violence if we're going to bring race into it," Carl said rationally.

"Carl, race is always in it. We ignore things and act like we don't hear it every weekend we ball, like we're some great melting pot basketball crew. A direct illustration of what I'm saying is just how Carl referred to Julius. He calls Julius Jules and he calls Perry Pear. When he explains things to the black guys on the team, he refers to them as brothers, but we should all be your brothers. You make it really clear where your love and loyalties are," Manny went on to explain.

"Are you serious right now?" Carl asked with a look of discombobulation on his face. "Damn right," Nick chimed in. "Look, I know Steven, Manny, and I are the guys that you work with. I also understand you've known many of these guys since you were kids, and I get you're from the same environment. Even still, the relationships may be different, and rightfully so. We work together, spend personal time outside of work together, and work as a unit on the court when we ball. I just feel like there should be a bond that's different but equally important. Don't get me wrong, Carl, you're cooler than a fan, but just like Manny said, you make it clear the different levels of relationships when we're all around each other," Nick continued.

"Fellas, that's not at all the way it is between us," Carl said, "and if it comes off that way I apologize, and going forward I'll be mindful of it. But it sounds like you guys have labeled me as a closet racist, or like I don't have the ability to be unbiased. That's a low blow, and it's certainly not indicative of who I am as a person."

Julius immediately followed Carl's statement: "It's stupid and immature is what it is. Black people can't be racist anyway."

Carl turned to Julius and immediately stated, "I'm not saying that, Jules. Please let me speak my own words."

Manny walked over to Paul's truck to grab another beer from the cooler, shaking his head.

"See, it's that kind of mindset that keeps that prejudice bull going on in this country," Silva stated.

"What the hell are you talking about? Are you trying to speak on behalf of African Americans and what we've been through since we were brought to this foreign land?" Paul interjected.

Carl let out a sigh of frustration, knowing Silva's statement only added fuel to an already inflamed situation.

"So, when you say we were brought to this foreign land, are you speaking about you specifically, because that tragedy took place centuries ago? You can't hold every white person or non-white person accountable for the sins of men that were dead long before you or I were even thought of, bro," Silva countered.

"See how they think? This foreigner swam over here willingly and illegally. Yet he feels he has the right to tell the story of African Americans without walking in the shoes of African Americans. Everybody wants to be black until it's time to be black. The light-skinned have adopted our style, culture, music, and our vernacular, but not the trials that a black man endures in this nation. Not only are you extremely removed from our plight, but you can't fathom what it means to be a black man in America," Julius explained.

"I agree with you wholeheartedly, but how do you have the audacity of accusing someone else of being a racist when you're making offensive statements like my people, Mexican people, swam over to this country illegally? That's offensive to me. I was born here, and if you hadn't noticed, brown people are not all that favored and privileged in this country either."

"Well, I don't think like that," Carl stated to distance himself from Julius's general critique of everyone not African American.

"Neither do I agree with that kind of thinking. However, I do side with Julius about you trying to speak like you understand the plight a black man faces in this country," Paul added.

"I'm not trying to act as though I know what it means to be black, because obviously I'm not black, but how long will black people use what happened centuries ago to be the reason for being held back in this day and age? I know racist people. Many are within my very own family, but I don't embrace that mindset. But I do get frustrated when I'm blamed for what white people did generations ago, and when I hear the race card being used as a trump card in every situation," Steven said without hesitation.

"So, wait, black people use the race card to address every situation, is that what you just said?" Milo asked after remaining silent the entire time this discussion had been in progress.

"It's a bit of an exaggeration to say in every situation, but it does come up in a lot of cases," Nick added.

"Let me explain something to you that you may not know because oftentimes it's hard to relate to things that do not affect you directly. Allow me to help you to come down from victim status, by dealing with your level of frustration when black people bring up this so call race card. When you see injustice in the world, whether on the news, social media or up close and personal, if you do not speak against the injustices against black people, you my friend are part of the problem, and your silence gives authorization towards it. It's no different than having a married couple as neighbors, and you've heard and witnessed domestic violence from the husband toward his wife. When you look the other way and relieve yourself of accountability by saying, I'm going to stay out of their business, you're contributing to this form of physical abuse, as indicative of you cosigning on systemic racism," Milo said with passion.

"Oh wow, so not only am I a racist, I'm also a man who consent to spousal abuse," Nick yelled out of frustration.

"If that's what you took away from what I said, it's clear I have you pegged correctly, and you're quite delusional about the truth," Milo said.

Steven immediately cut in, "That's unfair for you to make such a broad statement about all white men. Are you saying that in the rash of police shootings of African Americans, I may as well have pulled the trigger because I didn't march and protest outside of a police station with African Americans chanting 'we shall overcome'?"

Julius immediately ran toward Steven in an aggressive manner, but he was grabbed and held by Carl and Manny to prevent a physical altercation.

Steven backed up several steps, frightened by the near miss.

"Let me go. I'm fed up with him and his racist comments," Julius yelled while struggling to break loose from the hold Carl and Manny had him in.

"Julius, please calm down. This is not the way. We can have this conversation, as uncomfortable as it may be, without resorting to violence," Carl yelled while being out of breath from his struggle to maintain the hold on Julius.

"I guess that's the white man's fault too that he's reacting in an aggressive manner. White privilege is to blame for his inability to communicate effectively without attacking anyone who disagrees?" Nick asked indirectly, but aloud.

"You're just as guilty as he is," Paul said. "You like to provoke Julius and other people because you know that kind of talk gets people riled up. That's the exact same thing the reality star you voted for does. You see, all this empty rhetoric about slavery and systemic racism being a thing of the past, it's just done in a more savvy, consequential way. There are good people in the world who are white, brown, black, and all other nationalities who stand for what's right and not just for who's right. The appeal using a coded language is for those who harbor this kind of hatred for black people, and minorities altogether. Non-whites who feel this way are foolish enough to think they are accepted, but in reality, they're tolerated because they coincide with the agenda. They're simply constituents, not comrades, pawns and sacrifices for the slaughter. Many of these people like yourself believe their mentality of hatred or their money puts them in an elite club that wants to, how does he say it, Make America Great Again," Milo continued in a calm but direct manner.

Julius regained reason, and Carl and Manny released him from the hold that had subdued him. Even Julius had to take heed of Paul's statements. Milo was usually a man of few words, but generally when he spoke, it held power and wisdom.

"Well, you guys can minimize all that's been said all you want. That was a great speech, Milo. I had no Idea you spoke so well. Did you get an athletic scholarship and benefit from some form of charity to get your education at one of the HBCUs?" Steven said with intent sarcasm.

"Actually, I did obtain a scholarship, but it was an academic scholarship at DePaul University. Nonetheless, it only paid my tuition and my residence on campus. I worked to pay for my books and to finance my partying ways by dancing exotically for your mother. She just couldn't get enough of this dark meat. I know the men of your culture have always been self-conscious that your women would journey to this side and never come back." Milo resumed, after letting Steven's putdowns arouse his anger.

"You son of a bitch, why can't you stick to your own kind? You guys always bragging about how curvaceous black women are, but they're truly obese. If they have such great bodies, then leave white women alone and stick to the artificial hair and eyelashes your women wear," Steven continued.

"See, that is why I wanted to put my foot in his behind parts. You guys keep holding me back, but you won't always be around," Julius pleaded.

"Oh, so your true feelings of how you really feel about black people are coming to the surface, Steven?" Carl inquired. "How many times have you said to me over the years that we're all the same color when the lights go out or we all bleed red. Numerous times I've heard you refer to black women in the office as being hot. Now all of a sudden, my sisters are obese with artificial hair and eyelashes. Let me tell you something. Every culture is different, and every man has his own taste of what he views as being attractive. I won't demean white women to retaliate against what you've said about my sisters. I'll direct my comments to you, because you're who I now have issues with. You're fake and you're phony. You're the racist type that tolerates African Americans in the workplace, and you're fascinated by our women and style. On the other hand, you have closet feelings that we're inferior to you. From this point on, we're colleagues who only communicate concerning the job. I would have more respect for you if you were an open racist, but you're a coward who's a closet racist. I've lost all respect for you. How can you spend time with and pretend to like people you have hatred for? You have absolutely no character, and you're the worst manner of a man walking the face of this earth," Carl stated evenly with conviction.

Julius smiled when Carl conveyed his depiction of Steven. The area remained silent for several moments. Even people who were not with their group and enjoying the sights of Lake Michigan were attentive to their display. Steven felt uneasy and exposed. All he could think of was how to escape at this point. "Think of me what you will, bro. I'm leaving, and just so you know, I am a Trump supporter," Steven said as he motioned for Nick to follow him as he walked toward his car.

But Carl had one final thing to say to Steven. "I already knew that, and although I'm not a supporter of his, I felt our political stances didn't have anything to do with our relationship and us respecting each other as men. I'm glad you had the opportunity to reveal who you truly are today."

Steven beckoned to Nick once again to join him in his departure. "Are you leaving with me or what, Nick?"

Nick shook his head and looked down at the ground instead of facing Steven directly. "I don't exactly agree with those sentiments. What you said about the women who work with us was disrespectful. Leaving with you now signifies I support that stance, and I passionately object to it." Carl was surprised that Nick didn't side with Steven, but he opted not to say anything to let the interaction play out.

"Oh, so you one of the brothers now?" Steven yelled from his car, with one foot inside his car and the other foot planted on the ground.

"Look, I know we've had conversation about black people religiously blaming historical things that have happened in this country, and integrating that into every current situation. Playing the black card is what we call it, right? But I am in no way, fashion, or form saying all of them are that way." Nick explained.

"All of who? I'm a little irritated with you guys making inflammatory comments about black people but never really clarifying what you're saying. If you're referring to black people, then damn it, say black people. When I'm referring to those who look like you, I say white people because I want there not to be any confusion as to who I'm referring too," Paul said with passion.

"See, that's the thing right there. Every disagreement or different view has to be addressed by getting aggressive. Why can't we have a disagreement without resulting to physicality?" Nick said.

Perplexed by Nick's statement, Maurice asked, "So, is that your perception of how all black people handle things?"

Nick didn't answer Maurice right off, and Maurice didn't wait to see if he would respond. "Has someone laid a hand on you out here?"

Nick didn't answer, but he looked over at Julius reluctantly.

"There are nine other guys out here, and five of us happen to be African American. Did you not see two guys literally holding Julius to keep him from placing his hands on Steven? If we were all violent, we wouldn't just stand by and watch, we'd join in," Maurice said. "Although, I do applaud your stance as opposed to your counterpart Steven, but I got news for you, pal. Your mindset is not very far from his, and what you stated is a clear example of that."

Julius didn't take offense at Maurice using him as an example to make his point. It did cause him to look at himself and realize he was feeding into the stereotype Maurice was balking at.

"Look, we came out here to talk about getting in these upcoming tournaments with plans to win one if not both. Now, it seems we can't get past the fact that our different cultures contribute to being biased to some degree. Everyone has something they're prejudiced about, and if you say you're not, you're not being completely truthful with yourself," Manny proceeded to explain.

"So, are you saying being biased is different than being prejudiced?" Julius asked Manny respectfully.

"Yes, I think they are different. Someone can have some biases based on misinformation or ignorance toward a person or a group of people. That can factor in the way they see and deal with people because of the inaccurate information. However, to place a label on people they hate based on the color of their skin, and having a mindset of superiority toward a specific culture of people, that's the mindset of a racist person, I believe."

Julius didn't challenge what Manny said, but tried to process it without immediately rejecting it. "Manny, I hear what you're saying, but I don't see it being all that different, unless I'm missing something here. Yes, one mindset is more dangerous than the other, but what it all boils down to is the treatment and ideology one has toward a group of people." Steven, who still hadn't left, leaned against his car, shaking his head at Carl's comment.

"Getting back to playing basketball, yes, we did come out here to discuss plans for the tournaments and to develop a strategy. Many of us were blindsided to find out select people in our group have been in the closet about how they feel about people of color," Carl said.

Silva immediately interrupted Carl: "Honestly, I think we all have some prejudices, as Manny so eloquently stated. That doesn't necessarily mean a person is a racist. Furthermore, we have men who play organized basketball in college, professionally in the National Basketball Association, and overseas. The makeup of their teams is supremely diverse. It's irrelevant that their teammates may be prejudiced, have political stances, or different religious beliefs. When they step out onto that court, they block those personal things out and function as one unit, a team if you will. Why can't we do that if this tournament is so important to each of us?"

It remained quiet for a moment before Manny's cousin Paco said, "That's true, and as men with children, how can we expect them to go out and conquer this world in spite of these societal challenges, when we can't come together twice a week to win that trophy? Hell, focus the same way you do when you go to work. We go in there and make our money to continue providing the lifestyle we've become accustomed to for our families."

"That's a good point. Let's get it done. I don't give a damn about your political stances or what type of comb you use. What I do care about is winning one of those tournaments and staying in shape so I can continue to get the ladies." Many of the guys laughed, which broke some of the tension in the atmosphere.

"So, are we doing this or what? We can be grown men about this and put what happened here today aside," Milo said.

"I'm not sure. I need to know if the guy in the trenches with me has my back," Carl replied.

"Man up, Carl. You're better than this. We can get this done without the reality show aspect of it," Maurice encouraged.

"What's the matter, Carl, are you that agitated with me that we can't play together now? You can work with a labeled racist but you can't play basketball with one?" Steven said, walking back over toward the circle the men were assembled in.

Unwilling to be the guy who couldn't rise above the infraction, Carl surrendered and, without ever looking at Steven, said, "Okay, if you guys are in, then I'm in as well."

Each one of the men learned something about some or all of the men they'd been playing basketball with the past two years. Most importantly, without verbally acknowledging it, they learned some things about themselves as well. Some of the men were enlightened as to new possibilities of how they could be perceived, and some of the men learned that despite hating a certain mentality, they themselves could give off that same kind of energy and treatment toward others. Moreover, many of the men now assessed their prior association as business with a purpose, who no longer viewed their relationships as confidants but constituents who shared a common interest. The brutal honesty of this unforeseen verbal altercation may have altered their relationships, but it gave them a new perspective on the naïve way they had viewed the nation we live in.

THE ISSUE OF *Sexual IMMORALITY*

CHAPTER 9

EDWARD LAY IN THE BED next to his wife feeling frustrated after having yet another night of unfulfilled physical intimacies. He and his wife Bethany had been married for twenty-two years, and their marriage was a model for many other married couples who were family and friends. Nevertheless, Edward desperately desired for his wife to perform in a way the women performed in the abundant amount of pornography he watched. Bethany wasn't open to the introduction of anything sexual except traditional intercourse with her husband on top of her. Edward was heading toward middle age, forty-nine years old and quickly approaching fifty. In past years he had been able to suppress his sexual frustrations, and primarily focused on their children and his career. With Edward and Bethany's children now being adults and only one of their children residing in the home, Edward found himself bound to the insatiable appetite of having sex the way he had become accustomed to for years, which was through pornography and masturbation. He desired to have sex the way porn turned him on, but his sexual drive had diminished as he struggled to accept the next phase of his life.

Edward had difficulty sustaining an erection without being fully stimulated by pornography. In the past he had been able to close his eyes and imagine the physical images of women he was attracted to when he would attempt to have sex with Bethany, but this was no longer an option.

"I don't know what you want me to do. Maybe it's time you talk to your primary care physician about Viagra," Bethany said, observing Edward's obvious frustration. Edward didn't respond. He placed both feet into his boxer shorts and all in one motion he slid into his underwear and turned his back toward Bethany. He yanked the comforter on their bed and pulled it over his entire body, exposing only his face. "Getting angry I'm sure only makes the problem worse. Why can't we communicate like mature adults?" Bethany waited for Edward to respond, but all she heard was mumbling she couldn't quite understand. "I don't know what you want me to do. I'm as ready as I can be, and I'm willing to help. You need to stop getting angry and just relax."

Edward turned over very quickly to face Bethany. "We've been married twenty-two years, and we've been together nearly thirty years. I don't want to talk and process things with you during sex. I want action. I'm probably the only man in the world that doesn't receive oral sex from his wife. If you're not going to please me, just stop talking and allow me to at least get some sleep."

Bethany knew his proclamation was the root of their bedroom issues. She wanted to satisfy her husband, but the things instilled in her by her mother, Gloria, early on weighed heavily with her. Repeatedly when Bethany was a teenager, Gloria told her that if she were to perform this kind of an act on any man, he was sure to lose respect for her and view her as a scarlet woman.

"You lied to me," Edward yelled as he repositioned the comforter and bed sheets.

"I didn't lie to you. You misconstrued my words, and you've been holding it against me ever since. Why can't we just be satisfied with regular sex?" Bethany pleaded.

Edward was referring to what Bethany had said to him when they had lived together for nearly eight years before they officially married. All three of their children were born prior to their union, and her family shamed her at every waking opportunity. Bethany finally succumbed to the pressures from her mother, aunts, and even some friends to give Edward an ultimatum. If he was unwilling to commit to her legally, she declared to him she would move on with their children.

"What's wrong with the way things are now? Half the people in my family that have married in the past fifteen years have filed for a divorce. Why put unnecessary pressure on our relationship to get a piece of paper to say I love you?" Edward asked.

Bethany frowned and explained out of frustration, "It's not about the paper, Edward. I've given you three beautiful children, and you haven't made an honest woman out of me. You know I wanted to get married even when we were in college."

Edward hesitated for a moment and finally said, "Well, there are things I want from you too, but you won't do them, so why should I be forced to give in to your demands when I can't have what I want?"

Bethany was well aware of Edward's indirect approach. "I am not a harlot, so please stop trying to strong-arm me to perform illicit sex acts. If that's what you want, then you go out and get a whore, but my children and I will move back in with my parents if you don't marry me soon."

Surprised by Bethany's demand, Edward responded, "Bethany, you know I love you and our children more than anything in this world, but I have needs as a man. Isn't marriage supposed to be about compromise?" Edward said, appealing to Bethany's conscience.

"Yes, we are, but there are some things a woman should only do with her husband. I have already disgraced my family and my church by having children out of wedlock, and residing under the same roof with you without a commitment."

Edward assumed Bethany meant she would be susceptible to his sexual fantasies when she spoke of things husbands were entitled to. "If getting married is the barrier to us going to the next level, we could go downtown this week, get a license and be married," Edward said urgently.

Bethany smiled but immediately stated, "I don't want to be married by a judge. I want a wedding, and I want to be married by my pastor in a church." Edward was known for being a penny pincher with money. Even still, he was a great provider and a good planner. He'd already saved money over the years for their wedding. It wasn't until two years ago that he decided to use those savings toward purchasing the classic nineteen-seventy Chevrolet Chevelle he so desperately wanted.

Edward and Bethany were married four months later, but as time progressed, Edward became increasingly ungratified and resentful toward his wife. Bethany only worked during summers at the park district in their community. All of her energy went into caring for Edward, their home, and their three girls. Once again Edward made an inaccurate assumption about his wife and their marriage. He believed that at some point when their daughters were grown and out of the household, he and Bethany could build the sexual chemistry he so longed for. Their daughters Sarah and Rosalyn were now both married with families of their own, and their youngest daughter, Patricia, who was currently working on her second degree after deciding she no longer wanted a career in child development, still lived at home with her parents. But between school and her exclusive relationship with her boyfriend, Greg, she rarely spent more than three nights a week at home.

The following morning, while Edward went through his morning routines prior to leaving for work, he purposely was quiet, and he decided to make his own coffee this morning rather than waiting on Bethany to make the coffee for him.

"I see you've made your own coffee," Bethany said when she entered the kitchen after being in the bathroom for almost half an hour. "I made your lunch last night. You have leftover meatloaf and potatoes au gratin from dinner in a Tupperware bowl on the second shelf of the refrigerator. Would you like me to make you some breakfast before you leave?" Edward placed a slice of wheat bread in the toaster, but neglected to respond to Bethany. He opened up his email app on his smartphone while waiting for his toast.

"I see that you're choosing to reside in immature mode this morning. Since there isn't anything I can do for you this morning, and you refuse to acknowledge me, I'm going back to bed before I get started on this housework. Bethany turned to exit the kitchen on her way back to their bedroom.

"You know, actually there is something you can do for me. Our children are adults and have lives of their own. There isn't very much housework for you to attend to anymore, so you can get a job." Bethany was astounded to hear this from Edward. Throughout their entire marriage he had continuously stated he didn't want her to work, only to take care of their family. It was at this moment that Bethany realized the depth of Edward's anger toward her.

"You know, our bedroom issues aren't all my fault. I may have some reservations with performing those fetishes you try to impose on me, but have you ever stopped to think that when you are unable to perform that I am frustrated as well? I don't always get what I want either."

Edward had been in denial about his erectile dysfunction issues that had persisted far longer than he was willing to concede. He had always blamed his and Bethany's sexual frustrations on her, because of her reserved lovemaking skills. Bethany's stating that she too was unsatisfied with his sexual output was a harsh reality to Edward. Angry and embarrassed, he exited the kitchen door on the way to the garage en route to work. Within minutes he entered I-55, the Stevenson Expressway, but instead of listening to his normal upbeat music to help energize him prior to going to work, Edward just contemplated Bethany's statements while he drove below the speed limit on the expressway. He wondered whether her words were in retaliation to him asking her to get a job now that all of their children were adults and had lives of their own. Edward didn't really want Bethany to get a job. His salary was more than enough to provide for their household, while still adding to their savings and retirement. He thought the directive he had given Bethany about getting a job would force her into indulging in the sexual lifestyle he so desperately wanted to have with her.

His feeble attempt to play mind games backfired, and he wondered how long Bethany had felt this way. He questioned whether she had desires to have sex with someone else, the way he secretly did.

Edward was a maintenance engineer at Englewood Pallet Company. He and two other engineers serviced the entire plant, which was mostly machine-operated after downsizing and laying off many longtime employees over the past five to ten years. His primary responsibility was to keep all the machines that made and recycled pallets running at all times. Edward and the other two engineers who worked for the pallet company most often had downtime throughout most working days if the machines or any other mechanical parts of the plant were working properly. Equipped with a company pager and walkie-talkie, Edward spent a lot of time in the cafeteria reading, and also in the finance department so he could purposely run into Nova, the office clerk who worked on the second floor. Edward was really attracted to Nova, and she knew Edward liked her. She was also aware that he was married, but that didn't prevent her from flirting with him and making him feel needed whenever he entered her department.

Nova was very friendly, and she was excellent with customer service. She was highly beneficial to the company, especially since she was the first person people would meet in person or by phone. Nova was forty-five years old with a noticeably stacked figure. More often than not she wore fitted dresses that complemented her curves and proportions all together. Nova flaunted her long hair, regularly parading different hair styles. People were drawn to her infectious personality, and she walked displaying an upright form that exuded extreme confidence. Nova knew that Edward made excuses to come up to the department to see her nearly every day. He would often come up the stairs leading to the floor acting as though he was assessing the structure of the building. He would walk over when Nova didn't appear to be busy and ask, "Is everything working properly up here? Do you need me for anything?" If there were any issues in the entire plant, Nova would be the one to put the work order in for one of the engineers to carry out. There was truly no need for Edward to take this kind of initiative other than to give him the excuse to engage with Nova.

Edward and Nova would engage in small talk when she wasn't busy. What he knew about Nova was that she lived alone, because both her son and daughter had their own apartments. He also knew Nova was a good cook, because over the years she had asked him to taste dishes she'd cooked and brought in for lunch. Nova had a discernible cleft in her chin, and her lips were full. Edward enjoyed talking to Nova not just for the conversation, but because he was fully enamored by her beautiful lips. Nova wore expensive perfumes and lotions that were intoxicating to Edward and kept him buzzing around her work area. When Edward would stand over her desk, he would bask in the sweet smells, savoring these scents that invaded his nostrils. Although Edward was very much attracted to Nova, he never crossed any lines with her in pursuit of extracurricular activities outside of work. Although extremely frustrated with his and Bethany's sexual limitations, Edward honored the vows he had taken with his wife.

Nova always liked attention, especially from men. She never crossed any thresholds with Edward either, but she flirted and enjoyed the special attention he paid to her. Every once in a while Edward would bring Nova a vanilla latté with a shot of espresso and a whole-grain bagel with light cream cheese. His excuse for this would always be that this was in appreciation for sharing her lunch with him. Truth be told, Edward would have loved to do more of this for Nova, but he didn't want to send any mixed messages to her or anyone else working for the company.

Edward was a good man who was entrapped by the perverted exposures of his youth. As a child Edward was intelligent, and he was also a mild-mannered kid who respected his parents. His mother, Bertha, displayed a tremendous amount of love toward him and his siblings, but his father, Melvin, was a disciplinarian. Edward's father wasn't a mean-spirited man at heart, but he was hell-bent on raising his boys to be men, and how he went about achieving this was in the same authoritative way that his father had bestowed upon him. Edward was the eldest of three boys. He was given more responsibility as the oldest child, and when his father was not present in the home, he was commissioned to conduct himself as the man of the house, but under the direction of his mother.

In the early eighties, the Midwest launched cable television for the first time, and his father, who enjoyed watching baseball games, purchased service from the provider at the time called OnTV. The subscription had one channel that showed movies twenty-four hours a day, but with the turn of a switch on the control panel, he could now view Sportsvision. This new sports channel allowed Melvin to watch Chicago White Sox baseball games, Chicago Bulls basketball games, and Chicago Blackhawks hockey games. In the evening after he'd arrived home from work, he would watch these games on his floor-model console in the living room of their house.

Edward's two younger brothers, Mark and Kenneth, had designated bedtimes on school nights. However, Edward, being the oldest and having proven himself with grades that were consistently above average, had established a no-bedtime policy with his father, as long as Edward maintained a B average or above in school and always woke up in time for school no matter what time he went to bed. Not too long after the younger boys went to bed, Melvin would watch his games and have a few beers. He would head to the bedroom to have sufficient rest for the next workday.

Bertha always went to bed early because she had the task of waking her three boys in the morning and going through the process of getting them ready. Generally, she would cook breakfast after managing the household, and then she would drive them all to school.

Melvin was unaware for an extensive amount of time of the fact that shortly after the postgame show of his games, Edward would turn the control panel back to the movie channel to watch pornographic films that aired at that time of night. Watching these adult films eliminated the innocence he had as a boy. He began to look at girls and women differently, and he eventually began to act upon the images he'd been viewing in these adult-rated films. As Edward advanced to different segments of his life, his appetite for sex increased after graduating to magazines with extreme nudity and hardcore sex videos that were now available for renting. For many years Edward felt deprived by his wife, because in his expectations of Bethany, his hungers were driven by the compulsive nature that had become manifest within him over the years. It wasn't until three years ago, when Bethany attended a women's retreat with a church their neighbor attended, that she finally came to some realization that Edward's perversion was his issue and not hers.

Typically, Edward's workdays ended at four o'clock, and on this day, he sat in the men's locker room while employees from the evening shift entered. Edward was viewing pornography on his cell phone with the volume muted to avoid being exposed.

"You must have some kind of terror for a wife. Several times after your shift has ended, I walk into this locker room and see you looking at that phone, clearly in no rush to go home," Byron, one of Edward's coworkers who worked the evening shift, said while he searched his locker for coffee filters to make coffee for his colleagues.

Edward laughed at the comment and responded, "No, it's nothing like that. I'm just in no hurry to dive into rush-hour traffic on my way home. If I wait around until about a quarter to five, traffic lightens up a bit." Guarded whenever someone journeyed near his pornography addiction, Edward had become good at lying off the top of his head, a practice he had perfected since his first exposure to pornography as a teenager.

Shortly after Byron left the locker room, Edward exited the locker room as well, and he was home in twenty minutes. As soon as he walked in the kitchen door he routinely used coming in from parking in the garage, Bethany ran into the kitchen and blurted with urgency, "You should clean up, and at least change your shirt. Your parents will be arriving for dinner in about an hour."

Edward's facial expression immediately changed, and the crinkle of his nose displayed his displeasure with Bethany's news. "Bethany, why would you invite my parents for dinner without discussing it with me first?"

Bethany walked over to the stove and opened the oven to check on her Roasted Cornish Hens and then she looked at her pots of pasta and spaghetti meat sauce before answering Edward. "I didn't invite your parents for dinner. I was talking to your mother on the phone and she spoke about how long it's been since she visited our home, or saw Patricia. She followed up by asking was it okay if she and your dad came by for dinner tonight to see us and Patricia."

"Did you tell her that Patricia is rarely home, and when she is, all she does is eat, sleep, and wash clothing?"

Bethany placed the two potholders on the kitchen table and stated in a matter-of-fact tone, "Of course I did, but apparently she had already spoken to Patricia, who agreed to be home for dinner if they were visiting. Your mother offered to buy dinner, but I couldn't very well have your parents in our home and have them eating restaurant food. They're guests in our home, so I'm cooking instead."

Edward shook his head in agitation. He was upset about this unexpected visit, but he couldn't be angry with Bethany even though he wanted to be. "Many days in the year Patricia doesn't come home to have dinner with us. Miraculously, she has time to have dinner with my parents without checking to see if we approve of the idea."

Bethany walked back out of the kitchen, but not without saying, "They're your parents, Edward. What do you expect her to do?"

Edward was noticeably seething. He hated things unplanned and on the spur of the moment. He especially hated feeling as though he was being bullied into conforming. Edward didn't have a problem with his parents coming to dinner. He just needed to be mentally prepared for the old stories his father liked to tell about when Edward was a kid. Edward felt these stories embarrassed him in front of his family, otherwise he would willingly invite his parents to their home more for dinner and events.

Edward took a shower and put on comfortable, casual clothing. After he finished freshening up, he vacuumed and organized the living room and the dining room, since Bethany was occupied with preparing dinner. The doorbell rang, and Edward looked at his watch. He hoped it wasn't his parents arriving. They weren't due for dinner for another forty-five minutes. He walked over toward the front door mumbling to himself, and encouraging himself that this engagement would only be for the next three hours. When he opened the door, it was his daughter, Patricia, who yelled, "Hey, Dad!" As she hurried right past him on the way to her bedroom, the coping methods Edward used to combat his frustration were no longer working, and he was angry all over again.

He sat down on the living room sofa and began distracting himself. He organized the remotes and magazines on the cocktail table. Within a few minutes, Patricia re-entered the living room. "I'm sorry, Dad, I had to use the washroom badly. I didn't mean to be rude."

Without looking up at his daughter, Edward stated, "Have a seat for a moment." Without hesitation Patricia complied. She knew whatever it was her father was about to say to her, it wasn't going to be a ball of sunshine because of the expression on his face. "Answer this for me. How is it that I never see you unless it's a Saturday morning when you usually sleep late into the afternoon, then wake up to wear down my washer and dryer the entire afternoon? By the evening you're headed out the door, and I may see you once in passing until the next Saturday afternoon. However, on a Thursday evening, you can be present for dinner because my parents have barged their way into my home. You never seem to have time for your mother and I this way. You're never home for dinner."

Patricia laughed at her father's indictment and responded in a casual manner. "I'm sorry, Dad, what do you want me to do? They're my grandparents." Patricia's answer to Edward's question was no consolation to him. Edward just shook his head and asked no further questions. "Where's Mom?" Patricia asked.

"She should be in the kitchen. Why don't you go and help her out? You know you could do something around here besides sleep and wash." The doorbell rang as soon as Edward was done speaking.

"But Dad, I'm never hardly here, but I'll get the door." Once again Edward looked at his watch. He was sure it was his parents this time, even though it was only six-thirty. Patricia opened the door and greeted and hugged her grandparents.

Bethany, hearing the doorbell, walked into the living room, assuming it was Edward's parents. "Hello, Mom and Dad," Bethany said as she greeted her mother-in-law and father-in-law with hugs as well. "You guys are a little early. The food is done, but give me a moment to set the dining room properly before you guys come in. Patricia and Edward will take care of you until I'm done setting the dining room for dinner," Bethany announced while walking briskly back to the kitchen.

"Edward, your family has greeted us, but you're standing there like you're waiting for a personal invitation to hug and kiss your mother." Melvin looked at his son with the same intimidating look that he used to frighten Edward with as a kid.

"Mom, you know I'm always happy to see both you and Dad. How are you two doing?" Edward asked and then kissed his mother on the cheek. He shook his father's hand firmly. "Come on around and have a seat until Bethany is done making a fuss over the dining room."

"Now, you leave my daughter alone. You're not going to find a woman who knows how to take care of a home like your mother and Bethany. They don't make them that way anymore," Melvin said and laughed at his own humor.

"Hey Granddad, I know how to cook and take care of a house. I learned from Mom, so all is not lost with my generation," Patricia said. Melvin hugged his granddaughter, who was sitting on the sofa next to him, once more.

"I'm sure Bethany has raised you to be a woman of valor as well, but these women today, all they know is how to stop off at some drive-through window, feeding these kids all this unhealthy food. Sarah brought our great-grandbabies over last Saturday to spend the day with us. She came in with a restaurant bag full of hamburgers and french fries. Your grandmother told her she would cook our great-grandchildren lunch and the restaurant food wasn't necessary. That youngest one, Mariah, threw a tantrum in my living room. She knocked over the pictures on top of my floor-model television. We watched Sarah have a full-blown conversation with a child, explaining to the girl she was out in public and if she wanted to go to the circus the next day, she had to stop misbehaving."

Patricia chimed in, "Studies have shown, Granddad, that disciplining a child rather than talking and letting them express themselves empowers them more than having them live in fear all the time. This better prepares them to succeed in the world."

"Says who?" Melvin asked. "Is that what they're teaching you in all those years of schooling you're getting at that college?"

Before Patricia could answer her grandfather, Edward stated, "You have a lot to say about how to run a household and how to raise children for someone who hasn't done either. All you know how to do is keep me working to pay for two college educations. You don't help with anything around here, so how did you come to know so much about how to run a household?"

"Dad, are you really going to start in on me? Grandpa Melvin and

Grandma Bertha didn't come all this way to hear you put down your youngest daughter. I'm sure Granddad extended himself for you before you figured out your way in life," Patricia added.

"You tell him baby-girl. The boy ate like a horse, and he always had some sort of football or baseball fees we had to pay."

Patricia smiled, enjoying the fact that Melvin was zeroing in on her father.

"Dad, that was in high school," Edward said, "and you made me take out student loans for my college education. I had a part-time job my senior year of high school, and you made me pay rent after I graduated. So please don't compare my life to my daughter's."

Bethany walked back into the living room and announced, "Dinner is being served in the dining room for you guys. The bathroom is right there for you to wash your hands, and Patricia, I need you to go downstairs and bring a bag of ice out of the deep freezer."

Patricia returned from the lower level of the house, and she filled everyone's glass with ice except for Bertha, who always liked her drinks at room temperature. Bertha sat down next to Bethany. "Your bathroom is always elegant, and it has such great fragrances every time we visit you guys. That's a new towel set, isn't it?" Bertha asked.

"Yes, mother Bertha, it is. I was looking for a shower curtain set that matches the new paint in the bathroom. When I saw the towel set, it complemented the shower curtain, so I had to have it." Edward placed two homemade biscuits on his plate and passed the biscuits to his father, who was sitting the next seat over from the head of the table.

"Patricia, my dear, what made you want to embark upon business administration as a major? You were excited about working with children before," Melvin asked.

"Granddad, it wasn't that I lost my passion for children or helping elderly people. Once I got into the field, I found out about the system. The state, if you will, provides limited resources for people on the level I was on. My superiors seemed more focused on staying within their budget rather than getting families what they needed. I had a situation with a senior client of mine, and they had a stint in the hospital because they were sad after losing a child to cancer. They were admitted to the psychiatry department for a month, which made them lose their apartment. I was instructed to send them to a nursing home in a crime-ridden community. I felt they needed to go to a detox facility to address the abuse of alcohol that contributed to the sadness, which ultimately led to the feelings of hopelessness. Nevertheless, I observed how some social workers would send clients to programs and communities that had way more resources. I came to realize just like in most communities in Chicago, the resources are not distributed fairly to minorities. On an administrative level I will be able to help people better rather than being handicapped by the biases of the system. As an administrator, I'll have some determination of how and where funds are allotted and how they will be used."

Edward looked at his daughter with intrigue. She had never articulated her overall purpose concerning her education to him this way. Edward would have understood Patricia's career change better if she had explained it to him the same way she just did to her grandparents.

"Dad, I know I'm costing you a fortune, and I know I was supposed to be done with school by now and out of the house like my sisters. I just couldn't see myself working a lifetime in a system where I couldn't make a difference on the path I'd chosen." Bertha nodded her head, acknowledging she understood where her granddaughter was coming from, and she was proud of Patricia for caring.

"Why did you decide to move home and live off campus this time, Patricia?" Melvin asked.

"Well, Granddad, it cost more to stay on campus while going to school. After returning to school after only one year in the social work field, I couldn't ask Dad to pay for the college experience I already had. I feel bad enough he's paid for two educations with me. The other determining factor was my first year I had a roommate who was beyond filthy. She smelled, never washed her bed sheets or her hair. She would eat chips and other foods, and leave crumbs and open containers lying around until the next day. I didn't want to live that way, so I had several arguments with her about how her lifestyle was imposing upon me, but it was to no avail, because she continued living in our dorm that way. I found myself cleaning up behind her. We lived together for two semesters, and as soon as I got used to just cleaning up behind her, she dropped out and I got a new roommate just as bad. She watched pornography constantly without shame, and nonstop she would masturbate. I'd wake up hearing her moaning and watching her sheets flap from her methodical hand movements. Overall, I loved the college experience, but I'm trying to be financially responsible with Dad's money, and I'm more focused on the education than the experience this time. It also benefits me to come home every night where I'm comfortable. Last time I was happy to be away from home for the first time. I now realize there's no place like home."

"Oh, my Lord, that young lady has absolutely no self-respect for herself. I can't believe she would do something like that in the presence of other people. What was her nationality, Patricia?" Bertha asked. Patricia laughed aloud before she could answer her grandmother.

"Mom, I don't think that's really the point," Edward said. "No matter her culture, the fact is it's totally inappropriate to do something like that."

Bertha quickly acknowledged what Edward said. "You're absolutely right, son. Her race has nothing to do with the act itself."

Melvin was already peeved with his son from a previous statement, but now he was furious. "I suppose you would take that stance about this sexual immorality since you engaged in similar behavior as a kid." Bethany and Patricia were stunned by Melvin's comment. Bertha was the only other person at the table who knew exactly what her husband was referring to.

"Really, Dad. You're going to bring up something in front of my family that happened when I was a child?" Patricia was curious to learn exactly what her grandfather meant by his comment.

"What am I missing here?" Bethany asked.

"My dear daughter," Melvin said, "my son seems to have everyone's number, and he behaves as if he has no issues, and he casts stones in everyone else's direction. But there was a time in his life when he wasn't so perfect in image." It was obvious Edward didn't want his father to continue, but he knew it would make him look even more blameworthy. "When I was younger and my three boys ate anything that wasn't nailed down in the house, I worked a lot of hours. My boys seemed to grow through the clothes I bought as fast as I could purchase them. As I stated before, Edward and his brothers were always involved in extracurricular activities at school. Rightfully so, because that is what Bertha and I both wanted for them. The activities just caused me to work more than I wanted to. I wanted to be at home more with my family, but my first priority at that time was to provide." Edward made an awkward sound indicating what his father was saying wasn't exactly authentic. "Chicago in the early eighties had two cable networks that were new to the Midwest called OnTV and the other company was called Spectrum. I decided on OnTV because other than the movie channel, it had what was called Sportsvision. I was able to watch Chicago White Sox games in the summer and Chicago Bulls games in the winter. I later learned that after Bertha and I went to bed, somewhere around eleven o'clock, the network would show adult films on this movie channel. Edward was the oldest of the boys, and as you know he has always been responsible. I allowed him to stay up as late as he wanted, as long as his good grades didn't suffer and he had no problems getting ready for school in the morning. One weekend Bertha and I went to a birthday party of one of my coworkers. When we came home, we entered the house to loud moaning sounds that turned out to be Edward fully engulfed in watching this kind of filth in our home." Patricia smiled. She was surprised to hear her grandfather divulge this information about her father. Moreover, pornography for her generation was easily available by way of the internet, and accessible on most smartphones.

"Patricia, can you please allow me to speak to your father? I really don't want you to be witness to what I have to say to him," Bethany asked.

"Sure, I'm done eating. I don't think I want to hear this stuff anyway. As always it was nice seeing you, Granddad and Grandma." Bethany was just asking Patricia to go into another room, but Patricia was leaving the house altogether, which was even more suited for what Bethany had to say. Patricia exited the house, jumped into her Grand Cherokee Jeep and sped off to her boyfriend's apartment. "Bethany, whatever it is you want to say or ask me, can we discuss it after my parents leave, please?" Edward asked calmly.

"No, not this time. What your father said has given me great insight into the deviant things you want to happen in our bedroom. Edward, throughout our marriage you've made me feel as though there was something wrong with me. You've made me feel inadequate and like I was incapable of satisfying my husband. What your father just conveyed about your addiction to pornography enlightens me to the fact that you were exposed to sex too early. Clearly that's why you have this perverted way of experiencing intercourse, when it was created to be beautiful."

Melvin was now feeling guilty for what he purposely exposed to Bethany, and Bertha couldn't help but feel this was a conversation Edward and Bethany should have alone. "I thank you guys for the dinner, but we should leave and let you guys discuss this topic alone," Bertha interrupted.

"Mom, Dad, you don't have to leave. In fact, I want you to stay. I now understand the root of my husband's issues, not to say I don't have my own. The thing is, he's always made me the heavy with our bedroom problems." Bertha was very uncomfortable, but she was planning to sit through it in support of her daughter.

"Bethany, is this really necessary to do in front of my parents?" Edward once again asked calmly.

"I believe it is necessary. See, Edward, I am not fragile, or incompetent in our bedroom, and I was never trying to deny you. Furthermore, what Dad revealed here tonight has brought clarity to me about us both. The labels and the mental abuse you imposed upon me was you not wanting to take a look at yourself."

"Bethany, you continue to use the word impose. You're my wife. Whatever you or I could do to please one another, it stands to reason that's what we're supposed to be doing. I never felt like you were imposing on me to go out and work consistently to provide for my family and maintain the lifestyle you have become accustomed to. Even now, when things are not quite right between us, and our children are adults, I abstract enjoyment out of taking care of you."

Bethany turned her chair so that she could directly face Edward. "Is that the reason why this morning you told me to get a job, because all of our children are adults now?"

Edward realized the words he used this morning were unsettling. He realized the impact now that he was no longer in control of his emotions. "Obviously, I was wrong for saying that this morning. I was out of line, so please forgive me. It doesn't excuse what I said, but I was angry about last night, and your attitude about it was detached. Now I've admitted that I was wrong, I've apologized for what I said, and I have asked for your forgiveness, Bethany."

"But can you acknowledge that your addiction to pornography has affected our sex life, and that this is your issue, not mine?" Bethany asked.

"Bethany, you view me as this ogre imposing his will upon you, when all I'm looking to have with my wife is the same as other married folks do." Edward was no longer tentative about discussing the issues of his sex life in the presence of his parents.

Bethany took a moment, as she appeared to be searching for the correct words to say. Nevertheless, when she began to speak, the cracking of her voice and attempt to hold back her tears displayed her hurt to everyone. "Edward, you have a point. I greatly apologize, and I ask you for forgiveness as well. I acknowledge that I do feel like my husband is imposing his will on me. I feel this way because my mother's stepbrother used to impose his will on me as a child by molesting me. I didn't have a voice then, and what felt like no choice as a child. Unintentionally, I've been quick to reject you, my husband. I exercised the power to say no to you that I didn't have when I was a child. The reality is I have to face the molestation that happened to me many years ago. You are not my violator, and I should have shared with you I was molested when I was a child. Edward was astounded by what Bethany was revealing, and it made him feel guilty and ashamed. He was now able to grasp how his advances came off to his wife. It was easy to understand why Bethany so often responded to him in such a callous way.

"Bethany, you have absolutely nothing to apologize for. I only wish I'd have known this pertinent information before today, but again I must take responsibility for not making you feel comfortable enough to be vulnerable with me. Vulnerable enough to share your suffering. Dad, I was angry with you earlier for bringing up the pornography situation in front of my wife and daughter. I felt it was a malicious thing to do, but I'm so glad you did. Throughout my life I have watched pornography, and until this day I never realized how much of a hold it has on my life. Regrettably, I've burdened my wife to perform in a way that had to be traumatizing for her. I take accountability for my actions, and I no longer blame my wife for my own issues of sexual immorality."

THE ISSUE OF *SELF*-HATRED

Chapter 10

The entire nursing home facility was somber after an intense meeting with the recently appointed facility director of operations chief, Bernard Williams. Bernard asked employees from each shift to come in an hour early to cover the patients in the facility as he had a mandatory one-hour meeting with shift employees. Bernard agreed to give employees who were scheduled off an additional day off the following week. However, the extra day off required employees to use their own personal time to cover for the day's pay.

Kymberly was extremely upset that she had to attend this mandatory meeting on her day off. "He's been the director all of six weeks, and he is getting on my bad side already. I was scheduled to have my car serviced today, and now it'll have to wait until next week for me to get it serviced," Kymberly stated angrily while talking to her coworker Beverly, who was just starting her shift.

"Well, at least you're getting another day out of the deal. That's one more day you don't have to be in here smelling old bottoms and urine," Beverly said jokingly. "I guess I shouldn't say that, even though I'm only joking. We're all going to cross the same road, God willing."

Kymberly gave Beverly a menacing stare before saying, "I am not about to endure you and that holier-than-thou madness today. Anyway, Mr.

Bernard better watch himself. Clearly, he doesn't understand the power of the Me Too movement right now. He even looks at me the wrong way, and he'll be answering questions from human resources and the Chicago Police Department."

Beverly was not in lock-step with the comments Kymberly made about their newly promoted director. Beverly was more optimistic for change after the previous director, Miles Ocampo, ran the facility based upon his own agenda. He showed preferentialism toward select employees who shared his culture, and any employee utilizing the union to file grievances became a target for retaliation. "I'll talk to you tomorrow, Kymberly. I need to get on the floor and check in with the patients I'm assigned to."

Kymberly immediately responded, "This job is not that serious, Beverly. These residents are not going anywhere, and clearly no one wants to be bothered with them."

Beverly did not respond to Kymberly's insensitive comment about the residents at the facility. Beverly only tolerated Kymberly because she was fun to be around outside of work. However, over the past year she had identified a lot of character flaws in Kymberly, especially in the way she treated the residents. Beverly was passionate and considerate to the residents of the Golden Life Nursing Home, because her own mother had required special care from professionals prior to making her transition.

Kymberly walked over to the nursing station to talk with one of the shift nurses by the name of Tala. "Ms. Tala, how are you today," Kymberly asked.

"I'm doing quite well, Kymberly. Did you have to come in for the meeting? I see you're not on the schedule," Tala asked.

"Yes, this guy Bernard acts like he knows what he's doing. I give him six months and someone else will be taking over that position," Kymberly said, continuing in her negative attitude.

"You look really nice with your new hair, and you must have a boyfriend who spends lots of money on you, because that watch looks expensive," Tala stated.

"Thank you, and actually, I bought this watch for myself. I had it on layaway at the jewelry store for about five months. I got it out yesterday."

Latasha, who was one of the CNAs at Golden Life Nursing Home, was within earshot of Tala's comment, and she found it to be offensive that Tala would imply the only way Kymberly could have such a lavish gift would be because she was in a relationship with a man. Latasha and Kymberly had started employment at the facility on the same day. They were in orientation together, but Latasha began to notice Kymberly having favorable interactions with a select group of people they worked with. It was evident in this situation as well. Latasha sat to the right of Tala at the desk, but Kymberly did not acknowledge her.

"I am bringing in soul food for everyone tomorrow, so don't concern yourself with bringing in lunch," Tala stated.

"See, that's what I mean. You have more rhythm than some of the people from my culture. Either you grew up around African Americans or you're having yourself a taste of one of our Mandingos." Kimberly added. They both laughed aloud, but Latasha grabbed her paperwork and removed herself from the environment. She was once again offended by the inappropriate conversation that was taking place in this professional environment.

"I need what I need, and I wasn't getting that at home," Tala responded.

"Well, I'm leaving. I'll see you tomorrow. Oh, did you want me to bring in some soft drinks since you're buying lunch?" Kymberly asked.

"Absolutely not. Save your money. I can use the receipts as a write-off for my other business."

Kymberly left the unit, and when she walked past Bernard Williams's office, he saw her and called her into his office. "Ms. Barnes, can I have a minute of your time to discuss some things?"

Kymberly was irritated by Bernard's request, but she did answer him. "Can it wait until tomorrow? You know technically I'm off, but you made it mandatory for me to come in for that meeting."

"Well, I'm sorry the meeting fell on your day off, but we all need to have the same information. I don't like secondhand information, and I'm not a fan of repeating things over. It loses its vigor from the initial offering. Besides, I just saw you laughing and fraternizing with Tala when you're off the clock. Surely you can spare ten minutes for me." Kymberly walked into Bernard's office and sat down in one of the two chairs that were in front of his desk. Her body language and facial expression clearly demonstrated she was unwilling to have this talk with him.

"So, what did you think of the meeting, and do you have any feedback that could be helpful?" Bernard asked.

"No," Kymberly answered abruptly.

"It's fine if you don't have any feedback, but I asked you two questions, Ms. Barnes," Bernard clarified.

"I really don't have anything to say concerning that meeting, Bernard.

There isn't anything I could say that will make a difference as to what you're doing around here anyway. If there isn't anything else, can I please leave now?" Kymberly responded with agitation.

"I'm sorry you feel that way, Ms. Barnes. I take everyone's feedback into consideration. I also would appreciate it if you address me in a professional manner by calling me Mr. Williams, with the same manner of professionalism I address you as Ms. Barnes. Please don't assume you can be so common with me that you neglect to respect the office I hold. Lastly, I called you into my office because I've had two complaints concerning your interactions with our residents. It has been reported that you speak to our residents with an attitude, and when they ask you for your assistance, you make them feel as though they are bothering you. I've also had one nurse complain about you discussing our clients' personal business in front of other residents."

Kymberly immediately chimed in, "The only nurse that would have said that about me has to be Apunda. She thinks she's better than everyone. She says African Americans do not know their culture. I don't like anyone looking down on me, and I'm not going to kiss her butt just because she is one of the charge nurses."

Bernard could not believe Kymberly was responding this way to the alleged complaints against her. What she didn't know was that the way she conducted herself in her response was giving the complaints made against her validity. "Actually Ms. Barnes, I don't particularly care about your personal feelings toward Ms. Apunda Olowe, or her personal feelings toward you. What I am concerned about is the level of professionalism, or should I say lack thereof. Our residents are the reason this facility exists, and they have worked their entire lives. They're seniors, and they will be treated with respect. This is not up for debate, and as mild-mannered as I normally am, I certainly have a low tolerance for any negative behavior in this community. Consider this a verbal warning to you, Ms. Barnes, and I highly suggest you contact your union representative to let them know that it has been issued."

Kymberly was seething after Bernard delivered his final blow, but she began to stand down from her original position, knowing that prior to Bernard's promotion, he was one of the shift nurses and witnessed first-hand Kymberly's interactions with the residents. "Thank you for letting me know. I will be contacting the union, and if there isn't anything further we need to discuss, I would like to leave now, Mr. Williams," Kymberly stated in a much calmer tone.

"You enjoy the rest of your evening, Ms. Barnes, and I will see you tomorrow."

Kymberly left the facility, and met her cousin Rebecca at Sweet Maple Café for brunch. Rebecca and Kymberly had a standing engagement to meet biweekly at select restaurants within a ten-mile radius. Two weeks ago, Kymberly had cancelled their brunch date because her coworker Tala had needed her to meet her at an Infiniti dealership to drive her to work, due to Tala's car requiring maintenance service.

Rebecca was already seated, the host of the restaurant having escorted her to the table. "I'm sorry I'm late. I had a mandatory meeting at my job, and then my new boss who doesn't know what the hell he is doing gave me a verbal warning after the meeting." Rebecca could see that Kymberly was upset, and she hoped they could discuss the cruise they'd been planning, but it was obvious Kymberly was in a foul mood.

"I thought you were off every other Wednesday. Why were you there for a meeting and received disciplinary? That's just short of Craig getting fired on his day off," Rebecca asked.

"I'm really not in the mood for jokes and all of your movie analogies, Rebecca."

Rebecca could already see how their appointed time together was starting off. She had been looking forward to sharing current news, and she hoped Kymberly approved of her restaurant selection.

"Hello, my name is Lynnesha. I will be your server this afternoon. Can I get you something to drink while you look over the menu?"

Almost immediately Kymberly responded, "I just sat down. I know you had to see that. Can you give me a moment to catch my breath before you start in on your desperate aspirations for a tip?"

Embarrassed by the way Kymberly spoke to the server, Rebecca apologized. "I greatly apologize. Can you bring us two raspberry iced teas and give us about ten minutes before taking our order, please?"

Lynnesha was offended by Kymberly's attack toward her, but she was able to quickly move past it because of Rebecca's acknowledgment and apology. "Thank you, ma'am. I'll be back shortly with your drinks."

Kymberly checked the text message on her phone she had received while driving, and then she stated, "Please don't apologize for me. I don't really feel the need to apologize to a waitress who doesn't possess the etiquette that her position requires. She just needs to play her position and stay in her lane, that's all I'm saying."

Rebecca stared at Kymberly for a brief moment while gathering her thoughts. "I get the fact that you've had a challenging morning, but treating people that way is something that I'm not into. If you are so distraught that you feel the need to be rude to people who don't have anything to do with the reason you're angry, we can truly have our brunch date at another time."

Kymberly acknowledged Rebecca's feelings about her behavior, and she could see she was offended. Normally, Rebecca was an even-keeled, mild-mannered person. "Rebecca, I already cancelled our last date. I do want to have brunch with you in this place. I've heard good things about their food. I didn't mean to embarrass you. I know how you are about treating everyone with respect. I apologize for my entrance. My morning and afternoon have gotten off to a rocky start."

Rebecca sat back in her chair and then stated, "Can we just enjoy brunch, and this time and space together? We already missed our last girl day because you had something wrong with your vehicle, right? Did you have it serviced?" Kymberly had lied to Rebecca previously, unwilling to acknowledge that she was cancelling their time together to help someone else get their car repaired.

"Here are your drinks, and I'll be back shortly to take your orders," Lynnesha stated as she set the two glasses of raspberry iced tea in front of them.

"Is this tea sweetened or unsweetened?" Kymberly asked.

"All of our teas are sweetened. I know some restaurants sell unsweetened tea, but we don't have unsweetened tea as part of our drink selection."

"Thank you," Kymberly responded in a condescending manner. As soon as Lynnesha walked away, Kymberly continued, "I asked her a simple question, and she goes into the history of teas sold in America. She seems quite pleased with herself for someone that waits on people for a living."

Rebecca once again stared at Kymberly after her demeaning statement. "You said not to be rude to the waitress. I wasn't speaking to her directly, I was talking to you," Kymberly explained, followed by laughter.

"Did you get some kind of promotion that I'm not aware of?" Rebecca asked.

"No, but I've been seriously thinking about getting into a nursing program. The CNAs do all of the work with the residents, but the Registered Nurses make all of the money. Anyway, why did you ask about a promotion?"

"I asked because I'm somewhat bewildered that someone who assists clients with bathing and changing of adult diapers as part of your work requirements has the gall to present this entitled mentality toward servers."

Kymberly didn't understand fully the point Rebecca was making, and she attempted to deflect Rebecca's point. "I hope you're not comparing what I do with this waitress whose financial lifestyle is totally dependent upon whether someone tips her or not. I have a career, I'm employed by a well-known organization, and I have a pension plan. Clearly the customers who enter this restaurant will not be contributing to her 401k plan." Kymberly then picked up her menu with high-spirited energy, indicating her statement was the exclamation point to Rebecca's account.

"Obviously you've totally missed my direction," Rebecca said. "It will be fruitless to entertain the matter further. Be that as it may, I will say this." Kymberly set her menu down on the table to give attention to what Rebecca had to say next. "I love you, and you are my favorite cousin. You always have been since we were children, and I pray you receive this with love and respect rather than misinterpreting the content of what I say. I notice whenever we venture out in public, your treatment and depiction of black people is really harsh. However, you tend to give other cultures the benefit of the doubt. You give them grace, but you automatically assume the worst of your very own people. It's a painful sight to see. I love you, and I just have to call you on it."

Kymberly was absolutely furious, but she refused to allow Rebecca to know that she'd rattled her cage. "If you really loved me, or respected me the way you say, you could never see me in such a vile way. I treat everyone as an individual. Most importantly, I treat people in accordance with the way they treat me." Kymberly rose from her seat, grabbed her purse from the chair next to her, and exited the restaurant.

Over the next few days, Rebecca tried to communicate with Kymberly. Notwithstanding, Kymberly refused to accept Rebecca's phone calls, nor did she respond to her text messages. Rebecca challenged Kymberly to move past her feelings and assess whether or not what she had said had any credibility. Unfortunately, Kymberly wasn't receptive to taking a look from another angle, and because it was Saturday, Kymberly was already in an unusual funk. The staff at Golden Life Nursing Home were mandated to work every other weekend, and this weekend for Kymberly happened to fall on the same weekend that Kendrick Lamar was in concert at the United Center.

Krishna, the property manager of the building complex she resided in, had bought tickets for them to attend. Kymberly had been flirting with

Krishna for more than two years. Since Krishna knew Kymberly was a big fan of Kendrick Lamar's music, coupled with the fact he was no longer in a relationship with his ex-girlfriend, Krishna finally got up the nerve to ask Kymberly for a date to attend the concert. She was infuriated that she had to decline his surprisingly wonderful gesture to buy concert tickets. She was even more disappointed that she couldn't attend after Krishna finally asked her out. Krishna was of Indian descent, but he'd been living in the United States since he graduated from Northwestern University approximately eight years ago. Kymberly tried to leverage the extra day off she had been promised after she attended the mandatory meeting on Wednesday, which happened to fall on her scheduled day off. Nevertheless, Bernard stated that her request didn't allow sufficient time to establish coverage on the weekend, which was always a staffing challenge.

Kymberly exited the parking lot adjacent to the nursing home facility. As she entered the side entrance of the building, she rummaged in her purse and her item bag in search of her identification card. Jason, the security officer working this location, waited patiently. "I apparently have forgotten my I.D. What do I have to do to get up to my floor?" Kymberly asked out of frustration.

"Well, policy says your director or your charge nurse must come downstairs to sign you in before you can enter the facility, but if you give me your phone number and let me take you out sometime soon, you can go right on up on the elevator. I already know that you work here."

Kymberly's facial expression changed instantaneously, and her top lip curled in unison with her crinkled nose. "What would ever make you think that I would want to go out with someone like you? You are hardly my type. You sit down on a stool all day checking identification cards for hours. What would we have to talk about? That's really not a conversation piece. Can you please just call my department and go about your little security guard business?"

Jason was resentful of Kymberly's rude attitude toward him, but he remained professional and followed through on the correct protocol to minimize an escalation. When Jason completed the call to Kymberly's department, he relayed the information given to him by the unit secretary who answered the phone. "They're telling me that the charge nurse from the previous shift is currently giving handoff report to the oncoming shift, and they say the charge nurse for your shift hasn't reported for duty as of yet."

Unsatisfied with Jason's report, Kymberly responded, "So, do you think I'm going to stand here looking at you all evening? You already stated you could confirm I work here when you were trying to make your advances toward me. Can I just go upstairs, please, before I'm late clocking in?"

"I've already explained to you, ma'am, that your manager or one of the charge nurses has to come sign you in. I'm sure once the morning charge nurse is done giving the handoff report, she will come downstairs to sign you in."

Kymberly instantly retorted loudly, "So, because I won't go out with you and your little feelings were hurt, you're going to be an ass about the situation."

Jason did a double-take after hearing the profanity Kymberly used toward him. "There's absolutely no reason for you to become verbally abusive toward me for simply doing my job. Can you please step to the side so I can service other people entering the facility?" Kymberly glared at

Jason for a few seconds, then proceeded toward the elevators. "Ma'am, I need to either see an I.D. or someone must sign you in." Kymberly ignored Jason, and when the elevator doors swung open, she entered and journeyed up to her department.

As soon as the elevator doors opened on the third floor, Bernard Williams was entering the elevator as Kymberly was about to exit. "What are you doing here? It's the weekend," she said.

Bernard smiled before answering Kymberly. "Soni asked me to come down to the lobby to sign you in when I entered the unit. Tala will be thirty minutes late for work. Soni cannot leave the unit unattended without a charge nurse, so I was on my way to sign you in. Did you find your I.D.?" As soon as Bernard questioned Kymberly, the other elevator doors opened and three security guards exited.

"Oh, there she is right there," Jason said.

"Listen, ma'am, if you cannot show us a Golden Life identification card or have your director and/or charge nurse sign you in, you're going to have to leave the facility, or we will have to call the police to have you escorted off the premises," Carlos, the sergeant and shift supervisor, stated.

Kymberly was stunned by the turn of events happening right in front of her boss, but she still could not bring herself to accept responsibility for how she was handling the situation. "Did he tell you he was going to let me on the premises if I agreed to go on a date with him? He's only angry that I stood up for myself like women all over this nation right now." Sergeant Miller, who was Jason's superior, looked over at him but didn't offer any response to Kymberly's accusations.

"Listen, I'm Bernard Williams, and I'm the Director of Patient Care

Services. I will come downstairs and sign her in. Can she please report for duty while I come downstairs with you?" Bernard asked, while showing Sergeant Miller his I.D.

"Yes sir, that will be acceptable, but we still have to fill out an incident report and name you in the report," Sergeant Miller explained.

"That's quite fine. Whatever protocol that must be followed needs to be carried out to completion," Bernard said. He turned to Kymberly. "Oh, and after you swipe in, make sure you get a report from someone on the previous shift. Come to my office afterwards, please. I'm here this weekend to complete annual evaluations before the time period elapses." The elevator doors closed with Bernard and the security guards in transit to the lobby.

Kymberly clocked in as instructed. She was sixteen minutes late at this time. She entered the unit and located Soni, the morning charge nurse, to receive her assignment and the community report. After receiving her assignment and report, Kymberly journeyed to the women's restroom first after being informed by Tala, who had now arrived for work, that there were bagels and donuts in the breakroom that she had brought in. When Kymberly entered the breakroom, her coworker Beverly was making coffee for everyone to go along with the donuts and bagels Tala had bought. "Hey, Kymberly, I see you're here today, so I guess they couldn't find coverage for you to go to the concert tonight, huh?"

Kymberly set her carrying bag and purse in one of the breakroom chairs and walked to the other side of the table to open one of the boxes of donuts to make her selection. "Exactly. They didn't accommodate me obviously, and I really am trying to keep it together, because my mind is on this beige complexion of a man with a sexy accent right now. The last thing I need today is to be in here dealing with these Medicare recipients."

Beverly wasn't going to endorse Kymberly's negative depiction of the residents they served, so she simply stated, "They're just adult babies that need the love they've given to everyone else for years. Have you looked at the assignments?"

"No, but I have it right here," Kymberly replied. Beverly gave Kymberly a peculiar look while she turned her back to add coffee to the filter in the coffeemaker. "This is some bullshit. I should've just called in and followed my first mind. I'm missing out on my date, I can't see one of the most talented artists in music, I had an incident with security that made me late for work, and to top it all off they've given me pissing Gladys when I was assigned to her yesterday." Rhonda, one of their coworkers who was also a CNA and in the break room, laughed at Kymberly's rant.

The breakroom door swung open, and Bernard walked in. "If half the staff members are in here fraternizing and eating donuts, who is servicing the residents we've been entrusted to care for? And when I said for you to swipe in, get report and come to my office, Ms. Barnes, that didn't include you coming into the breakroom to take a break before you even start working. Can you come to my office, please?"

When Bernard left the break room, Rhonda offered a helping hand to Kymberly. "I'll cover your clients while you're receiving your evaluation, but this is not a good look right before your performance appraisal."

Kymberly was dismissive of Rhonda's comment. "Whatever. I don't anticipate that he'll last long in his position anyway. He doesn't know what he's doing, and his annual review of me cannot be too accurate if he's only been the director for just over six weeks."

"Why do you keep saying that about him? Can we at least give him an opportunity to succeed at the position? He can't be any worse than the director we had before who only cared about the well-being of his own countrymen," Beverly asked out of frustration.

"I'm having a hard time understanding what all of that energy was about, but we can revisit that after I go see Bernard," Kymberly said prior to exiting the break room. As soon as Kymberly entered the floor, she was informed by one of the other nurses, Rachel, that her assigned resident Gladys had another episode of urinary incontinence. "Tell Rhonda. I'm going to Bernard's office for my annual evaluation," Kymberly sounded off without looking at Rachel prior to exiting the department.

Bernard Williams's door was open when Kymberly stood in front of his office door. He did not see her standing there because he was immersed in an urgent email he had just received. Kymberly knocked on Bernard's door lightly. "Come on in, Ms. Barnes, and have a seat. Give me sixty seconds to respond to this email, and we can begin your performance review." It took Bernard three minutes to reply to the email, and when he looked up, he saw Kymberly texting on her cell phone. "Are you really sitting in front of me utilizing your phone when you know policy states you're not to use personal devices in patient care areas?"

Kymberly placed her phone in the side pocket of her scrubs before stating, "This is not a patient care area. You called me over here to conduct my review, and you're making me wait while you're playing on your computer." Bernard looked at Kymberly but didn't offer any response to her limited insight. Her comment was only confirmation of his personal assessment of Kymberly. "Here is your performance review. Look it over, add any comments you may have in the comments section, and please sign at the bottom," Bernard said as he placed her performance review document on the desk in front of her.

Kymberly attentively read her performance review, and within seconds, her facial expression changed. She continued reading until she had read the entire review. Kymberly set the paperwork in front of Bernard while brandishing a sly grin.

"Can you please sign it at the bottom, please?" Bernard asked.

"This must be some kind of joke, right? Do you really believe that I would sign such a blatant display of inaccuracy?"

"Ms. Barnes, if you don't agree with something in your review, there are sections to make your comments under my review comments."

Almost immediately Kymberly responded angrily, "On almost every section of my review you stated that I did not meet expectations. Guess what, you don't meet my expectations either. That position you're in is like a revolving door. I've been here seven years, and you're already the fourth director we've had. You wouldn't know that because you've only been here a year-and-a-half, and in this current position less than two months. If you think I'm signing that, you'll just be waiting, because I will be calling my union representative," Kymberly stated with irritation.

"If you don't want to sign the performance evaluation, sweetheart, you don't have to, but there will be a write-up for using your personal device while you're on company time, and for failure to display a Golden Life identification card that signifies to our patients that you work here."

Kymberly rose to her feet and yelled, "Oh, and I am not your sweetheart. When I contact my union and my attorney, I will also inform them that I was sexually harassed while I was in your office." Kymberly exited

Bernard's office with confidence. She was sure she had the ammunition needed to seal Bernard's destiny, with him still being under orientation review as the director. She assumed her accusations would cancel out any disciplinary action Bernard was planning for her.

The shift wasn't as eventful as most weekends were, and when the end of the shift was winding down and all of the residents were in their rooms sleeping, the staff benefited from this unusual quiet time to complete their paperwork and engage in small talk. "Rhonda, thank you for covering my clients earlier and changing Gladys for me. That was a big help," Kymberly stated.

"No problem, and you're welcome. That's what we're supposed to do for one another, right? Anyway, how did your annual review pan out with Mr. Williams?"

Kymberly spun around in the office chair she was sitting in to face Rhonda. "It didn't go well at all, but after I report him for sexual harassment, he will stand down."

Beverly was sitting two seats down from Kymberly charting on the residents she was assigned to this evening. When she heard what Kymberly said, she chimed in, "You seem to have some sort of problem with black people, and I'm not sure you're even aware of it."

Stunned by Beverly's bold statement, Rhonda moved out of the way so that Beverly and Kymberly could communicate without an obstacle in their view.

"You know, you said some disrespectful stuff to me earlier in the break room," Kymberly said, "and now you're trying to front me off in front of everyone. I highly suggest you be mindful of what it is you say to me.

This job won't save you from the repercussions of fronting on me." At this time everyone that was either talking in small groups or completing their work assignments was attentive to the situation at hand.

Beverly responded, "If that was some mindless reference to engage in some sort of physical fight with you, I am not intimidated by you, and I decline your small-minded offer."

"Ladies, I need you to remember you're at work, and to remain professional. We still have a few residents that are awake, and please don't put me in a position to have to deal with any incidents I'll have to report." Tala stated.

"There won't be any incidents on my part," Beverly said. "I will finish what I want to say to Kymberly, but it will be appropriate because I have the ability to articulate in such a way that I can communicate my feelings without resulting to acts of violence." Tala looked over at Kymberly after Beverly's declaration, and then she calmly walked back to the end of the nursing station to continue her work.

"Was that supposed to be some subliminal shot toward me, Beverly? Anything you have to say to me, you don't have to code it. You just better watch the way you deliver it to me, though."

Beverly smiled but offered no response to Kymberly's passive-aggressive threat. "Anyway, that comment you made about Mr. Williams and your plan to make accusations of sexual harassment. It's girls like you that overshadow women who have really been victims of sexual harassment. I despise women like you who are merely opportunists. Furthermore, your plan to take down a man of color using the Me Too platform will never materialize, because I've been witness to you saying you would do such a thing a few days ago, just because you had to attend the mandatory meeting. With our previous director, it was clear he was biased and looked to elevate and protect those of his descent. The moment a black man gets promoted, you can't wait to bring him down with such a malicious accusation." Kymberly was stunned and now even embarrassed as she looked on with no form of response. "What's the problem, Kymberly, do you hate the skin you're in? It seems that every person who's of lighter pigmentation, you give the benefit of the doubt, but you give my people a hard time. When other nurses who are African American assume to be in charge, you challenge their authority and their competence. But whenever Tala orders you to do something, or another non-black who's in charge for the day, not only do you carry out the order, but you do it while singing and tap dancing. I've watched you come in to work countless times bringing in food for the Asian or the white nurses, but I've yet to see you bring in anything for the black nurses or the nurse techs." There was movement by those within the nursing station which indicated there was validity to what Beverly was saying.

"That is not true at all. I don't go around buying lunches for people based on race," Kymberly said, trying to deflect from the hot seat she was in.

"Nice try, Kymberly. When was the last time you dated a black man?" Kymberly became increasingly agitated after Beverly's last question, because she knew that Beverly was privy to the answer. "How about you learn from the very people that you place in such high regard? They protect and look after their own. Why don't you learn to do the same?" Beverly politely rose from her seat, walked over to Tala and informed her, "I'm going to check on my clients, and then I will be taking a bathroom break if that's okay?" Tala didn't face Beverly, nor did she break stride from tapping on the keyboard of the computer. She simply answered, "Okay."

After Beverly exited the double doors that led to the restroom, Kymberly stated, "Misery loves company, but I know who I am." None of the nurses or the nurse techs engaged her statement. Kymberly for the remaining moments until the overnight shift arrived tried to appear unbothered by all that Beverly had said to her. But she did revisit the similar statement her closest family member had said to her just days ago while they were in the restaurant. Unfortunately, the painful reality was that Kymberly was unwilling to acknowledge the content of the truth conveyed to her. She embraced the image of who she thought she was, and continued in the downward spiral of her glaring, *unresolved issues.*